Here's To Old Friends

& New Lovers

Here's to Old Friends & New Lovers

By Qiana Watts

Also by Qiana Watts

<u>Memoir of a Love Jinn series</u>
Something Old, Something New
Tie the Knot
The Biggest Rock

<u>Cupid Heather Hanna series</u>
Cupid's Twist
Cupid and the Crown
Curing the Cursed
Cupid's Christmas Angel

<u>Cupid Lorelei Amoretti series</u>
Cupid's Sister
Cupid's Final Arrow

<u>Cupid Sonya Love Amoretti series</u>
Cupid Inundated
Cupid Goes Fishing
Cupid and the Rams
Cupid Tames the Bull
Cupid's Fun with Twins
Cupid and Crab Turmoil
Cupid and the Amorous Lion
Cupid and the Born Again Virgins
Cupid Meets Her Match
Cupid and the Widowed Scorpion
Cupid's Straight Shooting
Cupid and the Three Silly Goats
Cupid's Independence

ONE

I stared at the screen of my laptop between appalled and intrigued. Normally I don't open any of the crazy email offers in my personal inbox but the subject of this one kinda got me.

"Authentic Adonis dried sperm. Proven to draw suitors."

First of all it was first thing in the morning and a Monday. I was still percolating chai tea in my home office Keurig so I don't know what I was thinking opening the email. No chai tea in my system typically meant that I wasn't awake.

Second I glanced at it and even left the room to let Damascus out. I could have deleted it when I came back into the office but I didn't.

Instead I stared at the email and decided to Google it to see if there was such a thing. The email showed a picture of this guy lathering the dried sperm on various body parts. There was also testimony from a woman who swore drinking it worked better.

Most people would have been like gross! And I was. But I was more between yuck and fascinated. Who would think of selling dried sperm? Who would find someone to say that they drank it?

I grabbed my full glass of chai tea from the Keurig half paying attention. I blew on it finally deciding that it truly was a sham. I was completely gullible before my tea.

I deleted all of the crazy mail looking for anything valid in my personal inbox. Damascus scratched at the back door and I got up to bring him in. He trotted in front of me back to the office. He took his normal perch on the loveseat. He made one huff and took a nap.

"So I guess you're not helping me out today? We have a lot of work to do." I said opening my business email and my web site and my planner.

Damascus didn't look up. He might have raised an eyebrow if he had one. He obviously didn't care about any possible dilemmas I might be having. He *did* appreciate the silence of his morning naps though.

No sooner did I start my day than reminder alerts started popping up. On my iPhone. On my email.

I rolled my eyes and dived in.

You see I'm a wedding planner/matchmaker/travel agent. I own my own business called Eden and I love it. I'm a romantic and apparently this was a job I was born to do. Seriously!

Why?

Because I was apparently born a love Jinn. I was named after the love Jinn that lead to me: Jinx. I know! Great, huh? Jinx the love Jinn.

According to my protector Grey there might be six love Jinn in existence. I don't know if that's true or not.

Mostly it was cool to be a Jinn. I could grant my own wishes . I could make love happen for others.

I sniffled, suddenly seeing blurry which meant I either had a hangover or I was going to cry...again.

Then I stifled a whimper so I didn't wake Damascus but it didn't stop me from gut wrenchingly crying.

"Why can't I have love? I want that too!" I sobbed, pulling open a drawer in my desk for tissues.

On top of the box was a card that usually accompanied floral delivery. It was the card that came with some of the flowers Andrea had sent for my birthday in August. I reached down to pick it up and read it but at the last moment I changed my mind. I was already upset enough, reading the card was only going to make it worse.

I grabbed some tissues, blew my nose and got back to work. Of course I wondered if I would ever stop crying over Andrea. After all the break-up (if I can call it that) was all my fault. I could have been selfish and grabbed my man and hightailed it (where did that saying come from?) out of there and let fate takes its course. But nooo! Not me.

Briefly I should tell you that Andrea is a dude (because I'm not that sexually adventurous. Obviously. Who else would be staring at a dried sperm ad?). He was my first real boyfriend and the cousin of one of my former clients. He was hot to death (to quote my cousin and best friend Violet) and he was Italian (like born and raised. Like came to America on trip here with me). But he was also like the equivalent of a prince in the gargoyle world (nation? Tribe? Cult?)

Yes I said gargoyle. Some people think they draw weirdos to them. I know now for a fact that I do. Grey equates it to being a Jinn...on some levels. On other levels Grey can't figure out how nine Jinn before me never had the issues I was having.

So short story short (because I had only known Andrea maybe a month) I had to give him up to some unknown gargoyle chick so their clans wouldn't slaughter each other. The only consolation I got out of it was that when I wished away his memories of me I kinda told him where to find me again. But I didn't leave a phone number or anything. I just told him to look for a Jinn in Florida.

Stupid? Yeah I know. Welcome to my world.

Bing!

I jumped in my desk chair not expecting my Skype account to alert me of an incoming call. Shit! I wasn't presentable to anyone but family this morning.

My nose was still running from crying. I had no makeup on (which I do from time to time). I was wearing a T-shirt from St. Thomas, some boxers (not shorts) and my hair was still wet from my shower. I might or might not have brushed my teeth too (I know no one can tell that over the phone but it lead to my feeling pretty and ready for the world).

Bing! It should again.

I double tapped the screen with my plug-in play mouse for my laptop to see who was calling.

"Edwin?" I uttered in confusion, accepting the call without video (Genius!).

"Good morning, Edwin. How are you?" I greeted while I looked around for his file. I thought I had it out yesterday because I needed to work on it today. I found it on top of my filing cabinet.

"Is there something wrong with my camera? Can you see me? I can't see you." Edwin inquired in his soft Irish brogue.

"I can see you. It's just that I'm not presentable today..." I chirped opening the file in front of me.

Yeah I could see him just fine. A beautiful man looking like Legolas's father in The Hobbit: Desolation of Smaug. Edwin was unbelievably handsome like Andrea; which meant he wasn't normal. And Edwin Vaskaya wasn't normal. He was an Elf that lived almost all of his life among humans (meaning his ears were docked not pointy).

Edwin paused a moment on the screen. He had a gorgeous view behind him. He must have been at work or something. Then he laughed.

"Women. I should have thought about that before I decided to Skype. Maybe I should have had Solange call. Women don't mind seeing other women when they aren't presentable."

"No. We're worse." I admitted, hovering over his image on my screen and allowing video on my end. Might as well let him see me as I was at nine in the morning.

At least that's what I thought until Edwin backed away from his screen wide-eyed.

"Gee! Thanks Edwin. I'm not an Elf. I don't wake up looking gorgeous like you probably do. And I'm working from home today instead of one of my offices." I remarked in my own defense with a little lie.

None of my clients knew (well except for my first and only vampire client) that I worked from my home office in the house I now rented alone (thanks Violet!) in Jacksonville, Florida. My web site and business cards boasted several national and international offices that existed from time to time. My main mailing address was a private post office box in Orlando (where I've never lived) and that mail gets forwarded to me in Jacksonville.

The little deception was great for my business and I would do anything for Eden.

"On the contrary I was gobsmacked at the sudden image of you and for you to be so lovely so late in the day. You are at your home? Where? Italy?" Edwin apologized moving himself closer to the screen again.

Where was my imaginary home base again? Orlando? Madrid? I just knew Jacksonville and Karaj, Iran and Cairo, Egypt couldn't pop out of my mouth (originally I was born and raised in Karaj and then moved to Cairo and Jacksonville; but no one knew that).

"Actually I'm on a brief holiday in Miami. Nothing beats November in Miami. It's still eighty degrees here. But I thought I'd get some work in." I said casually, running a hand through my wet hair.

Did he say I looked lovely and I had just been crying? This man was a saint or he was blind. I'm going with saint on a shitty Monday morning.

"I've always wanted to go there. I've seen pictures of their beaches. So was I interrupting to call?" Edwin responded politely. He was always polite when we spoke.

"No. Actually I was just going over your file to see where we were when you called. Great minds must think alike so I'm told." I smiled glancing down at the checklist in their file briefly.

"Oh good. Solange wanted me to tell you that the invitations were all received and she will have a final count on guests on the morrow. Her major concern is the gown. She's received the updates that you have been forwarding to me. She would like to try it on before the wedding." Edwin gushed awkwardly because he probably felt like the middle man.

While Edwin was an Elf that lived in the modern world his bride to be Solange was not. She lived in Aucquince, an Elfin village in a massive tree outside of Ardee, Ireland in County Louth. She knew about modern stuff but she had no use for them in Aucquince. But Solange was a doll and completely worth the trouble Edwin had to endure I'm sure.

"A final fitting? Absolutely! I always suggest one especially when we are talking about

13

a one of a kind handcrafted gown." I stated emphatically, moving down my checklist to put an asterisk next to Final Fitting. I suggested final fittings but sometimes the bride or someone in her party decide against it.

"Would you be able to schedule that before the rituals? It's in less than two weeks..." Edwin asked moving emotionally from awkward to nervous.

I glanced at my planner at November and yep! The waning moon was closer than that.

"Then I guess I need to get off the phone with you and get to the nitty gritty." I said cheerfully, although I was panicking too. How did this thing sneak up on me?

Edwin chuckled and let me go.

Then I popped my Bluetooth into my right ear and spent the rest of the day busting my butt.

TWO

By the time I mentally checked out to feed Damascus and walk him I had my flight reservations made. Solange's dressmaker Veronica was available to meet Solange and me in Dundalk next Saturday; the fifteenth of November. The ritual was five days later so I sent Edwin a message to forward to Solange.

I even started on my wedding day schedule for Edwin and Solange before I mentally clocked out.

While I walked Damascus I called my aunt Matana (or Mattie so she sounded anything but Arabic). My Aunt Matana was my aunt by marriage and she was married to my dad's brother Ashraf (or Uncle Ash). She's also my best friend Violet's mom.

To elaborate a little further (until I get to my quick call) Aunt Mattie, Uncle Ash and my eldest brother Taj and his family are my closest relatives. The rest of my family moved back to Iran more than ten years ago. Violet was my roommate until a month ago.

"I was just getting ready to call you. I just told your uncle that we haven't heard from you in a while." Aunt Mattie said cheerfully. I imagined she was staring down Uncle Ash as she spoke.

"Stop it. I just called you guys last week. Maybe you have me mixed up with Violet." I laughed off as Damascus barked at the dog going by us in a stroller. I never understood that fad – walking a dog in a stroller. Where does he potty?

Aunt Mattie thought about it for a minute.

"Oh! You did call last week about possibly dog-sitting. Was that right?"

"That's right and now I'm calling to let you know that I definitely need your help. I'm leaving for Ireland next week. I just made reservations." I nodded, nudging Damascus gently away from the lazy dog. Damascus was probably telling the other dog just how lazy it was. Or maybe he was asking if there were strollers for bigger dogs like him.

Damascus was still a puppy but I could tell he was almost full grown. Damascus is a beautiful black Russian Caucasian Mountain dog. I encourage you to look him up. He's my dream dog.

"This wedding planning really makes money?" Aunt Mattie asked sounding really surprised.

Ten years ago no one in my family thought my business plan would work. My parents wouldn't even bankroll me but ten years later I'm doing alright for myself. I'm not millionaire that's for certain.

"Just enough. I have a wedding next week and I have about fifteen lined up. Which reminds me…Great! Aunt Mattie now I'm back in work mode and I just clocked out!" I huffed, hurrying our walk up so I could go home and check in on Mr. Parisi.

She said OK and that she couldn't wait to see Damascus. Then we hung up.

I got back to the house I rented from a family friend, poured a glass of peach Moscato (my new favorite) and went back in the office.

I spent the next hour fussing with Mr. Parisi to choose a resort. Mr. Parisi was a stubborn old man but he was a good man (somewhere in there). He was one of my Portuguese clients from my matchmaking service and now I was working on his wedding.

"I don't feel comfortable having some stranger help Cici and I with our vows." Mr. Parisi finally admitted probably pouting. From what I remember about Mr. Parisi's profile picture he looked like the American actor Jack Lemmon.

I feinted a gasp of surprise. Mind you we were speaking in Portuguese.

"Stranger? Mr. Parisi, I'm sure the event coordinators at these resorts are highly adept and pleasant."

"Are any of them a nice girl named Jinx Heydan? If they are Cici and I will choose." Mr. Parisi remarked offering up a rare compliment.

"What were you going to do on the river cruise, Mr. Parisi?" I asked muting my phone to say 'aw, he likes me.'

"Nice girl but stupid. You're a wedding planner, right? I expected you to see to the details. That's what. I'm an old man. My time is precious." Mr. Parisi grumbled. Back to his normal self in under ten minutes.

"I understand. Let me check my schedule to see what I have available before the end of the year." I said still remaining pleasant. It was Monday night. I wasn't missing anything on TV to rush off the phone.

Mr. Parisi grumbled and muttered away while I opened my planner again.

December was looking promising. I had a bridal convention, a final fitting, an appointment to find a dress and another to find a dressmaker. Not too busy. Of course Hanukkah was smack dab in the middle of the month. Ugh!

"Would New Year's Eve be OK?" I asked him hopefully.

He stopped grumbling. I sincerely hoped he didn't drop dead on his end.

"Just think. You could wake up New Year's Day with the love of your life. That would be so romantic, Mr. Parisi." I added in the silence.

"You make it happen. I'll have Cici choose the resort," he stated abruptly, hanging up.

I wrote Parisi's wedding in my planner on New Year's Eve. Then I definitely closed up shop for the night.

"Did we think of flowers?" Solange asked me as we climbed into Edwin's Jaguar to head to Dundalk.

I had been in Ireland two days. The first day I got re-acquainted with Edwin and Solange. I basically got drunk though with Edwin and his brother out in a tavern in Ardee. Solange went home early to deliver a baby (seriously! She did! Apparently she's a midwife of sorts).

The last time I was in Ireland I stayed in Aucquince. This time I found a cute little inn to stay in Ardee.

"Did you want flowers? Flowers weren't on either list of traditional or modern. Candles were." I responded drinking heavily from my bottled water that I got when I was out for breakfast. Hydration solved all hangovers. Unfortunately though I don't know where I learned that (possibly Violet? One of my brothers?).

Solange got behind the wheel, turned the key in the ignition and pulled away from the curb in front of the inn.

"I have got and idea. Do you want to hear it?" she asked me a few minutes later.

"Of course!" I expelled to sound enthusiastic. I was in 'encourage and support bride' mode. I found that both brides and grooms needed encouragement days before nuptials. Brides usually a week before. Grooms the day before.

"There's a candlemaker in Aucquince that can make them with flowers..." Solange said timidly, glancing over at me.

"I love that idea! Where do I find this candlemaker?" I asked genuinely loving the idea. I took out my phone to make a reminder for myself.

"Really?" Solange uttered in surprise.

I said really and she told me that she would be able to take me to the candlemaker when we got back from Dundalk.

And we did.

But first Solange and I saw her wedding gown all in one piece for the first time. Veronica delicately removed it from one of those dress boxes that you only see in Gone With The Wind. She handed the gown (that looked shimmery in person) to Solange to take to the only dressing room in the shop.

When Solange came back out she was in tears.

"I love it!" she explained wiping the tears away with her hands. Happy tears.

"This is the finest silk from Japan. They make kimonos with it there but I thought I would make a very intimate and sexy wedding gown." Veronica explained to us, eyeing Solange in the gown with intensity.

The silvery white gown was very sexy indeed. In truth it looked like a slip. The silk was so fine it was almost transparent. And the only thing that detracted from the slip was a tiny braided rope that Veronica also made. The rope would be tied around Solange's waist as she entered the ritual. During the ritual it would be tied around Edwin *and* Solange.

Veronica and Solange asked my opinion and I just whipped out my iPhone to take pictures. After I got my pictures I expressed my delight by asking Veronica if she could draw up a period gown for a wedding I had in England. She said she would get right on that.

I paid Veronica from the budget Edwin gave me. Then we took the gown with us back to Aucquince.

By the evening of the Elfin wedding ritual everything was in place.

The evening was clear. Solange's three sisters; Arabella, Kundry, Lyones and I laid out the lilac and navy blue linens on the lawn behind Aucquince (which was a city inside of a massive magical tree if I didn't explain that before). The three inch in diameter white wax taper candles infused with lilac and blue peonies were lit on the corners of the linens and within the sacred circle where Edwin and Solange would kneel.

I had checked with the caterer a few times who was set up in the city main square for the celebration dinner. They were set with a very cool vegetarian banquet.

So at half past nine when the moonlight was just right Solange eased past all of the guests sitting on the linens to gasps and awes. The trust stood in front of Solange and gestured that she could kneel already.

OK. Right there let me just explain from the Elfin scroll what was happening in regular people terms.

Solange chose to mix a traditional ritual with a modern one. In both (like I said) candles were required whether the ritual was done during the day or night. In both invitations were sent on tea leaf paper. And all rituals (regardless of what it is for) were presided over by a member of the trust; or a few members of the trust.

The trust were like religious priests or something. The ones in Aucquince looked like Lady Galadriel, Lord Elrod and some other blonde haired dude.

In a traditional Elfin binding ritual (wedding service) the marrying couple was naked. Modern ones (thankfully) allow clothing.

But during either ritual the highest ranking individual of the couple comes out first. In this case it was Solange since her family was held in high esteem in the Elfin world.

After they come out then the other individual (Edwin). The trust casts some spells, tells some predictions and then the couple are tied together by the rope. They are tied face to face for an hour to mind-meld or something. After the hour we get to eat and one end of the rope is tied to her wrist and the other end to his.

Traditionally there wasn't any ring exchange. However in modern rituals a small discrete token is permitted.

For Solange and Edwin they did rings that went on their middle fingers. I saw the rings over Skype before I came into town.

Anyway that's a Elfin binding ritual. And for my first it went pretty good.

"I'm so glad Henry recommended you. You were worth every cent." Edwin beamed when he and Solange stopped to talk to me at the celebration.

I had taken a post by the fruit cobbler deterring anyone from eating it (because after one bite I was hooked) when they found me.

I smiled sweetly at his compliment.

My black eyes kind of scanned the room before I responded unconsciously.

I almost had a heart attack though when I spotted Mor Keagh on the arm of Loghan Kerr.

Loghan Kerr was how I found out I was a Jinn.

"How did he get invited?" I growled, giving him the "eye".

Solange and Edwin located who I was staring down. Then they looked back at me.

"So *you're* the reason he got in trouble..." Edwin said with a sly grin spreading across his face.

THREE

So you guys know?" I asked a little nervous. Did everyone know I was the reason Loghan got in trouble? And why did Edwin say it like Loghan got his hand slapped or something?

Edwin and Solange gestured that we should move out of sight to speak privately.

"It was a mini scandal and no one would talk about the details..." Solange started softly, glancing at her husband to continue.

"All we know was that he had to get his Elfin affairs in order by the end of the year and then he would be ostracized from all Elfin communities." Edwin said with a shrug.

"But you didn't know why?" I asked hesitantly, glancing over their shoulders to see Loghan plain as day. What kind of punishment was that?

"Edwin's being kind. As always." Solange smiled blocking my direct view of Loghan for now.

"Am I? I'm not the one with an ear and voice in the trust." Edwin said kissing Solange firmly on the mouth.

"So what did you hear?" I asked her directly.

"Loghan hired a poor gargoyle boy who could see people's deaths. When the boy told him that getting married to Mor Keagh would end his second life prematurely he freaked out. For one Loghan already knew we were not supposed to look outside for answers. The trust told him he had a second life and he just wasn't satisfied."

"Then somehow he found out that a love Jinn could negate something or other. I don't know how he found out about you, to hunt you down. Anyway a few weeks after we all met and my uncle tells us (my family) that a Jinn protector showed up unannounced with Loghan at blade point." Solange gushed wide-eyed (which was creepy because Solange had cat pupils).

"The trust was more than happy to bind him to Mor Keagh, dock his ears and remove him from the population. They let Mor decide if a more just punishment should be in order. My uncle hasn't said if she had made a decision." Solange added after she caught her breathe.

"Why would Mor hurt him?" I asked curiously, remembering the strong independent Irish woman I met out in Ardee.

Mor was a little weird though. I remember she said she wanted absolute privacy and seclusion once a month. I didn't ask why. She was an Elf and that seemed to make the difference to me when I was matching them (I didn't know then that Loghan was a bogus client).

Both Solange and Edwin leaned closer to me at the same time.

"Mor is a sorceress," they said in unison.

"Sorceress? Not a witch, a sorceress? Sorceress implied evil. Is she evil? She just seemed eccentric to me." I asked skeptically, unable to spot Mor over the newly bound couple.

"There's been rumors of unfortunate events that befall her male partners. Right, Edwin?" Solange hissed, nudging her husband.

Suddenly I remembered what Mor had said about a previous marriage gone wrong. I caught that the husband died but...She killed him? Uh uh!

"Well there is a reason why she couldn't get the trust's blessing. And she does solely live in the mortal world plain as day..." Edwin alluded but didn't definitively confirm or deny.

See! Just another reason not to listen to gossip.

Just then a guest came up to give their blessing to Edwin and Solange so they moved on.

Then I was left to stare down Mor and Loghan as they made their rounds. I seriously wanted to walk up to them and give (at least) Loghan a piece of my mind. I even considered cursing him out in Gaelic just to be a bitch.

I took one step towards them and I was intercepted by Arabella, Solange's sister.

The first time I came to Aucquince I had tried to get out of here quickly and get back to Andrea; but I got suckered into doing a baby shower for Arabella. She was sweet and an Elfin baby shower is interesting to say the least.

"Need a ride back to Ardee?" Arabella asked me, jingling a set of keys in front of me. She and her husband gave me the ride to Dundalk where I met up with Andrea there after the shower.

"I haven't gotten paid yet…But ok." I shrugged figuring that Edwin and Solange were good people. I'd get my money.

"I've got your money, silly Jinn. It's bad luck for the newly bound couple to handle money in their first week of binding. It has been said to lead to horrible issues later so Edwin gave me the check to pay you yesterday. Come on." Arabella laughed, taking my hands to lead me away.

"Can you get me the recipe for that fruit cobbler?" I asked before I forgot.

Arabella laughed again and we left.

On the way back to Ardee she paid me and confirmed that Mor was a sorceress. Mor had been exiled for trying to create the perfect man and for trying to embody the Mother (which is their said "creator"). Basically Mor tried to play God and got in deep shit for doing it. But you got to love how she was exiled and lived about twenty miles away.

"The trust's hoping she does a little dabbling with Loghan as punishment. But I just learned that whatever elixir she's been working on to make the perfect man she's just used on Loghan." Arabella informed me as she walked me into the inn.

"So he won't die after all?" I asked between regret and disbelief. I never want anything bad to happen to anyone (hence the reason I'm alone and Andrea's possibly married) but Loghan Kerr? He deserved something bad for using Andrea and trying to make off with my cuff (that I was currently stowing in my lamp).

"No, silly. He's dead. The Loghan we see now died when she gave him the elixir. He's still exiled though. Elfin deaths can sometimes be spiritual. When you lose your soul you die even if breathe still fills your body." Arabella said with a smile.

Oh...kay...Creepy!

"That's a zombie in the other parts of the world, Arabella." I uttered hiding a shudder. I don't do zombies even though I'm a sci-fi and fantasy geek.

"In your world of humans you mean." Arabella scoffed. "Either way Loghan got what he deserved."

I decided to change the subject and ask about the family so I didn't walk away awkwardly. It turned out that Arabella and Roch were trying to have another child even though once she was pregnant they'd be separated (it was another Elfin custom).

I might have mentioned that because suddenly she needed to call home. Yeah! She loved her husband enough to give him another baby but not enough to be parted from him.

After she left I went up to my room to pack up and check my reservations for my flight home. I was flying out of Dublin so I had to go to bed early to get there in time.

<u>FOUR</u>

The next morning I was standing in front of the Starbuck's kiosk in the Dublin airport waiting on my chai tea. I was really tired and couldn't wait to get home to see Damascus. I still had a lot of work to do when I got home.

"Venti chai tea for Jinx!" the barista called out and I immediately rushed up to get it.

I did like I normally did with my chai tea. I held it close to my face and inhaled the warm spicy scent of the chai. Aw! Chai tea!

I didn't get a chance to take a sip before my iPhone rang in the pocket of my black slacks (they were comfortable and everything else I had needed to be washed or was at the dry cleaners).

I answered it as my tea and I headed to my flight terminal.

"How'd it go?" Violet blurted out in Arabic.

"Violet! How are you?" I responded back in Arabic. Arabic wasn't my first language just so you know. English isn't either. My first language is Far'si.

Oh boy! I should quickly explain that I pretend to be a born and raised American almost every day. Truthfully I was born in Karaj, Iran to born and raised Iranians. When things got sticky in Iran my grandfather moved everyone to Cairo (where Uncle Ashraf already lived). Then things started going bad politically in Cairo (so Grandpa said) and we came to Jacksonville, Florida.

So that's why Far'si (Persian, the language of Iran) came to me first. Although I can speak and understand any language that existed before the Tower of Babel til current as a Jinn.

"Tell me about the Elfin binding ritual first. It was in my planner." Violet insisted eagerly.

I told her about the binding ritual and the fruit cobbler while first class passengers were boarding.

"Oh! That sounds cool." Violet said passively. Which means that she didn't call to hear about the Elfin binding ritual. She called to talk about something else...probably herself.

"Where's Skylar?" I asked suddenly. I could have point blank asked her why she was really calling but that would be rude and mess up the game.

"He's around here somewhere. Why do you ask?" she said casually. I rolled my black eyes.

"Because he's your live-in boyfriend, right?" I responded like duh as my boarding was called.

"Yeah. Something like that. I'll give you a call when you get back to the States. I just missed hearing your voice." Violet said abruptly, ending the call.

"Uh huh, sure." I said to her but the line was dead.

Once I was on the flight and we could turn on our electronic devises I sent a text to Violet.

"What's really going on?" it said.

The in-flight movie was The Nut Job, which was a cartoon for kids. What about the adults? I pulled out the flier in the pocket of the seat in front of me to see if there were other entertainment options.

"Does it say there are any options?" someone asked from my left elbow.

I had the window seat which is how I preferred it. When we took off there was no one sitting in the middle seat or the aisle seat so I was genuinely surprised by the voice. I was even more surprised when I turned my head to respond.

"Are you shitting me? I don't see you for years and now twice in less than six months?" I expelled, hitting Violet's brother Mubarak in the face with the flier.

"I know. Amazing, isn't it? It's like fate," he grinned taking the flier from me and shaking it out to read.

I narrowed my eyes to glare at him. Mubarak and I didn't get along.

He perused the flier for a minute or two before he stuck it in the pocket in front of him.

"Why are you here? Is that even your seat?" I asked him folding my arms over my chest.

"Of course it's my seat. Do you think I would honestly purchase a seat next to you on purpose?" Mubarak retorted pulling a gray satchel onto his lap.

"Then where were you when we took off?"

"Offering my services to a first class passenger," he remarked bringing a tablet out of his satchel.

I didn't like how that sounded at all. But before I could say something else Violet responded to my text.

It was a picture and I was afraid to look at it for fear it was a picture of that stupid engagement ring. The first time Violet and I Skyped after she went back to Cairo she showed me a diamond ring that her ex-boyfriend Kyle Bach had sent to her with some stupid GPS coordinates.

I abhorred and detested (yes I know they mean the same thing) Kyle Bach. He was a bigot and the worst type of bigot. He didn't like Middle Eastern people but he was fucking my cousin and trying to speak Arabic to fit in. Personally he scared the hell out of me because he was in a position to do harm. Kyle worked for the FBI as an agent; which means he carried a weapon and could legitimately use it.

I handed my phone spontaneously to Mubarak.

"Can you tell me what your sister sent me? I'm scared to look."

"What? Is she sending naked photos to you now?" Mubarak quipped looking at my phone and then me. He didn't put down his tablet thought.

I glared at him again for his lesbian insinuation.

Mubarak took my phone, swiped, tapped and read (or looked at).

"It looks like a visa or something." Mubarak stated handing the phone back to me.

"Visa?" I repeated in confusion, looking for myself.

Sure enough it *was* a visa. I'd seen enough of Violet's work visas to know what I was seeing. However a work visa was the reason why Violet was back in her birth country. Her employer and the visa bureau didn't want to renew her visa again.

I typed back "another visa?" and hit send.

"What had you in Ireland, Jinx?" Mubarak asked a couple minutes later.

I was still waiting on a response while I stared at the little screens in front of me. A mole was about to give CPR to a dead squirrel from the looks of it. If I spend more time with Taj's kids like a good aunt I would probably know all about this movie. I was a horrible aunt and Taj did live close by too. Ugh!

"A wedding. That's what I do for a living after all. And you?" I responded casually hearing the refreshment cart somewhere. I still had my chai tea but a Danish or something would be nice on such an early flight.

"Seriously? People pay you to plan their weddings?" Mubarak laughed putting down his tablet finally.

I nodded, not wanting to go into my sales speech with dickhead Mubarak.

The flight attendant squeezed the cart down the aisle just then where I could see what came along with my ticket.

Scones! Nice!

She offered one to Mubarak but he waved her off. So I sat there enjoying my apple cinnamon scone waiting on Mubarak to answer my question.

Truthfully I didn't know what Mubarak did for a living. Whatever it was Uncle Ash and Aunt Mattie didn't flaunt or brag about it. And those two could brag. They tried to do it on the down low but I know they loved to tell people about their daughter the accountant as if they weren't impressive enough. Uncle Ask worked for some pricey finance firm and Aunt Mattie was a paralegal for an Egyptian law firm in Jacksonville.

I continued to stare at him until he answered me all the while eating my scone. Violet hadn't responded yet so why not stare down her brother?

Mubarak didn't get a scone but he did ask for black coffee; which he stirred oblivious to me.

"You're not going to answer me, are you? Come on! How can I still be a threat to you after all of these years?" I groaned in exasperation, giving up to pull my laptop out of my carry-on hidden between my feet. I never put my carry-on in the overhead like we were supposed to. Instead I had a very cool flight attendant tell me the trick I currently used. It probably was a bad idea but oh well!

"I thought we were still talking about you." Mubarak responded, finally taking a sip of his coffee.

I muttered a whatever as I waited for my laptop to load.

"Obviously whatever it is that I do my parents don't exactly approve," he remarked offhandedly, picking up his tablet again.

Then it dawned on me that Mubarak must really despise me. He was the apple of our grandfather's eye until I came around. Then his parents didn't approve of his line of work so he stayed away while I got to see his parents all of the time.

"So what is that? As if I care." I said just as breezily. Still no response from Violet.

"I'm a tattoo artist. One of the best in India and eastern Europe matter of fact." Mubarak stated with a bit of arrogance.

"Tattoos, huh? I remember you drawing. Aunt Emane bought you that sketch desk for your birthday once. I remember that." I replied finishing the last bit of my scone and tea.

Mubarak cut me a genuine smile that I caught.

"Is that something new? Looks like a tattoo?" he asked gesturing to my upper arm.

On my upper arm was the remnants of a burn scar from the cuff the first Jinx had made. He made two cuffs: one for him and one for his bride (who was a slave like him). However he was forbidden to do so and that's where the Jinn started. My grandfather (not named Jinx) gave the cuff to my paternal grandmother Nasira (his wife – questionably) to keep safe. When she died it came to me. Then it was stolen by Andrea for Loghan Kerr. It came back to me again and I stowed it in my lamp for safekeeping.

"It's a scar...still healing. Apparently I'm allergic to some metals." I lied.

Yes! I just lied to my cousin!

Mubarak eyed it and then dismissed it.

We fell into a comfortable silence for the remainder of the flight.

Violet didn't respond and I had to calculate what time it was in Egypt.

Mubarak and I parted at baggage claim where he was greeted by a Japanese chick dressed like an anime character. I assumed she was a girlfriend or something. She had a very colorful sleeve as it was called on one arm (I knew a little tattoo jargon).

So I left him to that and got my Jansport luggage (the best ever luggage in my opinion) from the carousel. I headed straight outside to got to the daily parking at the Orlando/Sanford International airport (sometimes I flew out of Jacksonville...some-times I didn't).

Unfortunately I stepped out into 110% humidity and shit if it wasn't November! That's serious climate shock when I left barely sixty degree Ireland.

My iPhone rang as I trudged through the lot to find my Altima (which only means I didn't shut off my phone when I told to on the plane).

It was Violet.

"Is it late there?" I asked her right away.

"Late afternoon. I didn't want to text this. Are you in the States yet?" she responded. I could see her shrugging in my mind.

"Yeah. I'm wading through my own sweat to get my car." I quipped spying several gray

Altimas but none of them were mine. What I needed was to put something distinguishable on my car that screamed Jinn wedding planner from Iran. Or maybe I could memorize my license plate number to save me the trouble because right now I was looking for the standard Florida plate declaring Duval County.

"Hmmm...that's not good. At least you don't have to travel with one of those chintzy fan water blowing things. Skylar carries a jug of water with him everywhere. It's really embarrassing." Violet replied probably wincing on her end.

"Yeah. They're probably calling him every name for Westerner. So what's up?" I laughed finally seeing a familiar dark gray Altima with a Duval plate. I took out my key fob and hit the trunk button. And it opened! Yay!

"That picture was sent to me by you know how with those coordinates again." Violet said like she was singing a tune.

I threw my bags in the trunk and slammed it shut. I unlocked the driver's side door by the key fob, preparing for suffocating heat as I got behind the wheel. And it was definitely a little thick in the interior.

"You know who? That's what we're calling Kyle these days? Does he say anything else in these messages to you? Like if he'll be there to arrest you for something crazy?" I remarked pushing the ignition button to start the car and A/C.

The Altima purred to life and I rolled down the windows. My purse was next to me and I was ready to head home to get Damascus.

"You just don't trust him, do you?" Violet huffed.

"Would you? Did he stop being a bigot recently? Never mind. Even if he changed his stripes yesterday I wouldn't trust him. And he's not my problem so I'll shut up now." I blurted out while I backed out of my space.

"He said you'll feel that way so he's invited you to accompany me to the coordinates. But he moved up the date." Violet said more than likely with a self satisfied smirk on her face.

"OK. I'll be there. Send me a text with the information. I'm about to leave the airport and I don't want you to hear me spazz out at the parking attendant when they tell me my bill." I said honestly.

Violet laughed and said OK.

I did spazz out when they told me the bill...quietly hyperventilating as usual. It was a little worse since I had made a scene in front of this attendant before. He just laughed in that partly amused sort of way, waiting on me to hand over my business credit card.

What I really wanted to do was add my parking charges to my planning costs.

Anyway I headed home after getting gas.

I got home with Damascus around four on Tuesday. We had dinner, took a walk and chilled out for the evening.

FIVE

Martinhal, right? You're sure now? Yesterday it was Belmar. The day before that was Yellow Lagos." I asked before I pulled out Mr. Parisi's file again.

It was Friday morning and time for my daily call from Mr. Parisi. I was supposed to be updating my blog according to my calendar reminder. But no...Mr. Parisi still couldn't make up his mind after I gave him a lengthy breakdown on all of my choice Portuguese resorts.

Really I should have known better. I was dealing with Mr. Parisi, the same man that took three years to figure out that I knew what I was doing.

Mr. Parisi grunted and groaned on his end.

"Oh! I don't know! This is women's work!"

So why are you trying to control everything? I was thinking it but I didn't say it.

"Then I'm going to hang up and talk to Cici...OK?" I said instead.

Mr. Parisi grumpily conceded, hanging up.

I dialed Cici at her daytime number. Her profile said that she owned a small florist shop in Oeiras outside of Lisbon.

"Adolfo couldn't make up his mind?" Cici said immediately upon answering.

"I think he might leave it to us now, Cici. So I'm calling to ask about which resort would you prefer I contact to set up the ceremony." I sighed hoping I didn't sound aggravated.

I stood up to pull the Parisi file off of the stack on the filing cabinet.

"Most definitely Martinhal. It has something for all of the family. Secretly I have took a trip to the property since our time is short. You know less than two months?" Cici said cheerfully and whispering like she didn't want anyone to know.

"Don't worry. We can get it done. Since you are a florist would you like to do the florals?" I smiled.

No lie within thirty minutes Cici and I had the time in mind. We did a conference call with a nice event coordinator Michel (who was a guy) who helped us lock in our date and time. He also sent both Cici and I menus form the resort catering department.

When the half hour was done Cici and I made an appoint-ment to speak next Wednesday about the dress. In the meantime I was going to select a few invitation styles and send them to her for approval.

I spent the remainder of my day working on that, my blog and new clients on my dating site. Most of my wedding clients were once clients that I matched together on my dating site (which is the same as my business site). So now you know how I got Mr. Parisi.

Right before I clocked out for the day my phone rang with a call from my current client Connie Rivas. Current meaning I was currently doing some work for them...namely their wedding.

Connie was a referral...kind of. I planned her cousin's wedding not too long ago in Colorado. It was up in the mountains and we were almost snowed in. But Connie found me at a Charlotte bridal show in July (I think). She was engaged to a nice Jewish guy and wanted me to plan her wedding. So far all I had done was go to dinner with the engaged couple and their parents.

"Did I catch you at a bad time?" Connie asked right after my very professional "Eden, this is Jinx Heydan" greeting.

"Not at all. I was contemplating eating real food for dinner or just a nice big glass of Moscato." I beamed knowing exactly who I was talking to because all of my current clients' numbers were saved under my Contacts.

"Oh! The Moscato definitely. Has it been a stressful day?" Connie laughed a little.

"No not at all. I end every day with a glass of wine. Wine and dark chocolate. But anyway...how can I help you, Connie? Unless you want to talk about wine and chocolate..." I laughed too, heading into the kitchen to find Damascus asleep on the patio. Apparently I had put him out an hour ago and got busy with three of my new dating clients (two were in Belarus. I never had any clients there so I was so excited to learn about them).

I opened the sliding glass door and stood there quietly waiting to see how far gone he was.

41

One ear perked up and then he stood up, came inside and plopped down again. My little man was either very tired or very bored. We needed some dog exercise or something.

"-so do you think you could?" I finally heard.

I had just completely zoned out a client! Oh crap! Play it off, Jinx! Play it off!

"In Charlotte?" I asked hoping Connie would tell me again what she needed.

"Actually in Atlanta. Josiah spends half of his time there. Eventually we're going to move there. But I think it would be better to find a photographer there. What do you think? I should be asking your opinion since you are working for me." Connie gushed sounding a little nervous.

"Oh! So you guys have decided on a destination wedding?" I gasped shutting the sliding glass door, locking and securing it before I went back into my office. One bad point of working out of my house was I couldn't escape work.

"Oh yeah! I knew there was something else I wanted to tell you. We decided to get married in Atlanta in early April. That just happened." Connie said with an awkward laugh.

I found Connie's file, grabbed a pen and wrote down Atlanta and April blindly.

"So you want to hunt down a photographer now?" I asked curiously.

"Too soon?" Connie wondered.

"Never too soon. People usually forget about getting a photographer until the last minute. When were thinking again?" I asked taking out my planner that basically held my life.

"Next weekend? Jos says that most photographers work weekends anyway." Connie said sounding a little less awkward. Maybe she was just busy or she thought she was asking stupid questions?

"I like Jos. He'll do right by you." I stated so she would know that I approved her choice for husband. That also bolstered a bride's self-confidence.

Connie said thank you and I could hear her smile. Then she said something about meeting at my office in Atlanta next Saturday morning before we headed out to shop photographers.

I said sure and told her that I would shoot her the address and time in the morning since I was sort of off the clock. She laughed and said shed be looking for a text or email.

I made myself a reminder in the morning to book an office suite in Atlanta on my Reminder app. Then I settled in with The Avengers on Blu Ray and a bottle of Moscato.

SIX

The following Saturday morning at eleven Josiah (or Jos), Connie and I met at my all beige office not far from the old Olympic grounds. Let's put it this way. I could see CNN Tower; which isn't saying a lot since (duh!) it was a tower.

I had already pulled my list of preferred photographers in the Atlanta area since I had done weddings here before.

"Strange…no color?" Jos remarked to Connie as I came out of the only office behind my leased receptionist Livia's desk.

Every time I rented an office space in Atlanta I always tried to get Livia Benson. I had done her wedding when I was first starting out. She's the one who told me about office rentals with staff since she worked for the company. So ever since she has been my go-to receptionist in Atlanta.

"I tried to let him know that we just relocated here." Livia stated as I passed. Always the story.

"Jos? You do interior decorating? What a cool hobby! Are you like David Brumstein on HGTV?" I gasped between teasing and flattery.

"I like to dabble. I don't have a signature style yet. My cousin does design though." Jos responded quickly, blushing a little.

"Don't listen to him. Right now our place is between space age modern and Western cowboy chic." Connie laughed standing up to shake my hand.

I got a mental picture and was just about to wince, giving a bad impression. Instead I chuckled softly. I had a problem with always showing what I was thinking on my face. Usually Violet was there to help me play it off; but she wasn't now.

"She's serious. But one day it might catch on." Jos admitted shaking my hand now.

I waved them back into the office, thanking Livia to be polite.

We sat down in the office. Me behind the desk, them in front of it.

Connie took a Galaxy Note out of her purse obviously prepared too.

"I hope you don't mind but I wrote down some photographers that looked interesting," she said tapping on her little tablet before she handed it to me.

I took out my own list that was in their file on my fancy rented desk (personally I liked my own at home). I perused her list against mine and we had a lot of the same picks.

"So how does this work, Miss Jinx?" Josiah asked leaning forward anxiously.

"Basically we go see these photographers. Do a little chatting. Check out their portfolio and take a business card and price list. Just leave it to me." I beamed enthusiastically, closing my file and standing up with keys in hand.

Unbelievably I didn't feel like flying to Atlanta so me and Damascus drove the six hours from Jacksonville in my dependable Altima.

Right now Damascus was chilling at a dog spa that I saw online. A lot of people rated it excellent but we'll see...

"But we can ask questions, right?" Connie asked as we headed out to the parking lot.

"Of course. You're the ones getting married." I smiled.

Once we were outside Josiah wanted to drive since he had programmable GPS (I just had Siri GPS). So I got in the back of the Sierra king cab and got to listen to meaningless polite chatter (all for my benefit no doubt). If I wasn't there they probably wouldn't have been chatting about Atlanta's shopping. They'd probably be talking crap about some family members or friend.

Anyway I let them chat like this for the first two photographers. But after a late lunch I decided to ask how Connie's cousin Frankie was on the way across town to Marietta.

"Did you match them or did you just do their wedding?" Josiah asked before his fiancée could say anything.

"Both..." I answered looking out of the window at some older African American man walking down the street. The man was wearing Red Velvet red from head to toe. And I do mean "head to toe". He had a red fedora, red suit, and red Stacey Adams. How does someone do that? It's so cool!

"Jos, you make it sound like you're accusing her." Connie slapped his right shoulder before she turned back to me. "We're not blaming you."

"What happened? They've divorced?" I asked anxiously.

"Oh they're still together..." Josiah remarked and I caught his smirk in the rearview mirror.

I was still confused, shooting a look at Connie.

"There's been a baby every eighteen months. Frankie's crazy in love with Luna. It's almost kind of disgusting." Connie told me with a wry smile.

"It's true love. True love should be eternal. Do you have pictures of the babies?" I beamed proudly. See! I was a good matchmaker.

Connie took out the Galaxy Note again to bring up pictures of her second cousins. She had stories to go with each picture which took us through the rest of the ride to Connie's choice pick for a photographer.

Jos parked and helped Connie and I out in the front of one of those boutique looking shops. We had shops like this in Jacksonville so I'm told (I never went). But I wasn't here to shop. I was here as a prospective client.

Jos let us into the photographer's studio like a sweet little gentleman.

Inside was very modern chic with black and white portraits and vivid color landscapes. It was ultra clean.

Jos and Connie started chatting with the assistant Jill who introduced herself right away. I checked out the works that were framed on the walls.

The black and whites were amazing. I had seen tons of photographer portraits in ten (almost eleven) years. I've had clients that insisted on black and whites. But none of the work I had seen previously compared to the work I was looking at right now.

"You can almost see the color, huh? It's the lens and the film. I even bought a new camera yesterday from overseas that should really make these pop," someone said next to me with a slight accent.

I know every language in existence like I said. I didn't know his accent; which was weird.

"It's not so much the color. I swear I can hear the scene. These weren't done in a studio." I remarked moving to the next portrait.

I didn't look beside me at the guy at my elbow. I was afraid. Something told me to be afraid, be cautious. And technically I was frozen in a good way (I was really amazed that I could speak or move).

Actually I hadn't done anything like I had just thought I did.

What I *had* done was look at the guy and OMG!

Andrea was hot and beautiful. Alexei who took me captive was very pretty too. Chris was attractive in a rugged sort of way. Even Grey was stunning (but he could be an ass).

48

This guy was heart-stopping. And my heart might just have stopped. My mouth did. It was just hanging wide-open.

"Miss Jinx? Are you OK?" Connie asked waving a hand in front of my face.

"Did you suffer a stroke? When someone spaces out like that usually it's a sign of suffering a stroke." Jos asked sounding like some sort of medical fanatic. Unfortunately medical fanatics are the ones that moved on from ER to Grey's Anatomy and really don't know shit. Besides Jos wasn't a doctor either last I checked.

Two things Connie's fiancé wasn't: a doctor or an interior decorator.

"I'm Rune Kalakos, owner and proprietor," the guy smiled, extending his immaculate hand to me.

I took it and shook it, willing myself to speak, move, blink. Damn! I think I could do that when I first saw Andrea. Gee whiz! You'd think I never left the house!

Please behave Jinx, I wished.

"Jinx Heydan, wedding planner and owner of Eden." I blurted out effortlessly with a bright smile. I even reached into my bag for my business card and handed it to him.

Rune took it, placing it in the pocket of his blue and gray argyle sweater.

"And this lovely couple are your clients," he smiled back. His teeth were extra bright and one of the top front teeth overlapped the other just a smidge. It was adorable. When I get a moment I'll describe Rune better.

"Connie Rivas and Josiah Cohen. We were hoping to take a little bit of your time to ask about your work and prices." I said professionally, nodding at the Puerto Rican girl and Jewish boy.

"First do you do weddings?" Jos asked because he just had to. I was glad Connie was marrying him and not me.

Connie rolled her eyes. "Please excuse Jos."

Rune shook his head and his thick brown hair barely moved.

"No?" Connie and Jos asked in unison, both confused.

"I do weddings, newborns, engagement photos and family portraits. No. I won't excuse Jos. Every man must speak his mind." Rune responded again with the accent.

"It's obvious you do weddings. The portraits on the walls show weddings." Connie remarked in a huff, crossing her arms tightly over her chest. Well not too tightly because her two karat diamond ring would have cut her.

Trouble in paradise?

"Come on, Connie. It's an honest question. Sometimes the portraits on the walls weren't always done by the photographer. Right, Mr. Kalakos?" I said trying to nullify or pacify the situation.

"Please call me Rune. And some photographers might do that. It's a fair question, Miss Connie." Rune said to back me up.

A couple minutes passed. The phone rang a few times and Jill answered it taking appointments.

Then Connie finally asked if we could see Rune's portfolio.

Again Rune shook his head.

"First I must take a picture of you. I feel that if you like the picture I take of you then I will show you my portfolio." Then he paused to retrieve his camera.

"Jill, get my portfolio out." Rune said to his assistant before he escorted us to the back of the shop.

The back of the studio had lighting and a simple black backdrop. So Rune must have done some studio work from time to time.

Rune had Jos and Connie pose and then re-posed them after he consulted with me. I think he was just humoring me. Then again I could have imagined the whole thing.

But twenty minutes later Connie and Jos loved their first picture done by Rune. We perused his portfolio in his private office also in the back of the studio. It wasn't necessary because I could tell they were sold on Rune.

"Can we speak with you, Miss Jinx?" Jos asked me in front of Rune.

Apparently they wanted to have a huddle so Rune excused himself to check on his next appointment with Jill.

"We like this one, Miss Jinx. Now what?" Jos asked leaning around Connie.

The three of us were sitting on the couch in front of Rune's (isn't that the coolest name?) desk. Connie was bookended by Jos and me.

Connie nodded.

"You guys tell me how much you want to spend on a photo-grapher and what you want him to do. Then I haggle to get him at your price." I told them, opening my file to flip over the previous vendor's price list. I was very good at haggling; besides anything left over my contract stated I could keep. It usually wasn't very much so don't think I'm robbing my clients blind.

"What did we decide last night? A grand tops?" Jos asked his fiancée, moving a piece of hair out of her face.

"A grand is fair, right, Miss Jinx?" Connie asked me anxiously. She probably thought Jos was being cheap.

I wrote a thousand dollars in brackets on my checklist next to Photographer.

"Perfect ceiling. Do you want him for the wedding and the reception? Will you feed him if he does the reception? If so is that to be deducted from his bill?" I responded crisply but with a pleased smile. These were the same questions I asked about every photo-grapher so hence they were on the checklist.

"Yes." Jos and Connie stated emphatically and in unison.

I took that to mean yes to all of the above so I checked the correct boxes on my checklist.

"And travel time? Do you want that included or excluded from the total price? Just in case he charges that." I asked next.

They waffled a bit on that and deferred to me. I told them I would negotiate if necessary. Then I asked how they wanted to receive the prints. These were all standard questions and would keep me from going back and forth between them and the vendor.

"Ok. I got what I need. Now if you could get Mr. Kalakos to come back in and you guys stay out in the lobby. It shouldn't take very long." I told them, standing up as a sign that they should.

"I'm so excited! Come on, Jos so Miss Jinx can work her magic." Connie clapped gleefully, hurrying to the door.

"Remember we're thinking mid April." Jos added before he left with Connie.

A few minutes later Rune returned after he knocked on the office door.

"It's your office." I laughed as he came in.

Until that moment I didn't realize how tall he was and I was five foot seven without heels. Today I was wearing jeweled bronze gladiator sandals for walking.

"I never want to scare you, Jinx," he stated causing a shiver to run down my back.

It was a good shiver. Not like the one Alexei gave me.

"That's nice of you. So let's talk business, Rune." I stated trying to keep on track which was hard when I noticed that he had blue eyes. Blue eyes and brown hair. Wow!

"I can't." Rune said simply, standing three feet in front of me but no closer.

"You don't want our business?" I asked blinking in disbelief. Usually they say no after I tell them my terms not before.

"If we talk business now I won't see you again for months, right? I might get a business email or two. Isn't that how it goes with wedding planners?" Rune asked with his arms folded over his broad chest.

"Are you asking me out? I know the words weren't said or anything but I'm also –" I uttered a little dumbfounded.

"A love Jinn and would be able to sense my attraction to you?" Rune interjected slowly beginning to grin.

Holy shit! Run!

SEVEN

The look of fright or flight on my face must have been evident like every other emotion I had because Rune closed the gap between us.

"Whoa!" Rune exclaimed holding me in place.

The feel of his arms around me didn't alarm me. I actually felt safe like in Andrea's arms. But oddly I saw my home in Karaj (the one place that I instantly melted into; moreso than Jacksonville). It was weird.

"I'm not for enslaving! I read it somewhere! You can't enslave a love Jinn! Borrow one...maybe!" I started screaming as Rune held me tighter.

He tried shushing me but I started screaming louder. No one came to my aid.

"Simmer down, little Jinn. No one is here to enslave you unless you want me to," he said and I'm sure he was grinning with his flirtatious comment.

My mouth fell open and I pushed against him so he could see my reaction to his audacity.

"Really? Is that how you talk to a client? I'm a lady too in case you haven't noticed." I huffed with a slight pout.

"Are we pretending again?" Rune asked with a mischievous glint in his blue eyes.

"I haven't stopped being realistic, sir." I retorted, putting my file back in my Michael Kors bag. Obviously Rune didn't want to conduct business!

Rune grabbed my hands, tugging me closer to his desk. He leaned against it, making him appear a little shorter. How damned tall was he?

"You are very stunning, Miss Heydan. Don't you think we have a connection?" he responded ignoring my rebuttals.

I wanted to lie but I blushed and I couldn't deny that I was a little taken with him. I shouldn't have been; especially since Andrea was still out there. He could have ditched his gargoyle bride and be looking for me right now.

Well too bad because I was in Atlanta right now, not Florida, my conscience scoffed.

"Wait a second! You're trying to bewitch me, aren't you? You're not really interested in me." I replied backing away, imagining a trap.

Rune pulled me back because I hadn't let go of his beautiful and soft hands.

"I was attracted to you the moment I caught a glimpse of you getting out of the truck. That was you, wasn't it?"

I eyed him skeptically. "You weren't outside when we came in."

"En contrare, mademoiselle. I was just returning from lunch when you three showed up. It was meant to be because I just had an appointment cancel when you came." Rune smiled and it looked genuine.

I still didn't believe him; besides...

"How do you know I'm a love Jinn?"

Rune held a finger to my lips.

"I'll tell you if you go out with me tomorrow. I have a wedding reception in the evening but I'm free during the day."

"You have some balls to ask me out." I said bluntly.

Rune looked down between his partially parted legs.

"I'm a man so I must absolutely have balls. Otherwise I'd be an eunuch. Then what pleasure would I have trying to please you in the future?"

I laughed before I realized it. This was incredible banter. It was somewhere between Andrea's intensity, Grey's arrogance and Chris' humor. I was riveted (seriously riveted).

"I love your laugh, Miss Jinx. Please let me spend time with you. If I'm a complete ass I will do business with you and leave you alone." Rune beamed letting my hands go so he could stand up.

"What if I don't think you're an ass afterward?" I asked, loving his smile. Already! I know!

"Then we'll have to do something about that," he answered with a shrug.

"You want me to think you're an ass?" I laughed again. I was uncontrollable.

"It sure would be easier. We would have an issue otherwise." Rune said.

"What kind of issue?" I insisted on knowing, hoping to keep the giggles at bay.

"We'd have to pretend to be strictly professional for your clients' wedding. Jos and Connie? Can you do that?" he said, unconsciously sucking on his bottom lip (I think).

Unconsciously I was staring at his lip now.

"Are you kidding me? I am exceptionally professional when it comes to making money." I stated regaining my composure.

Rune nodded affirmatively. "Do you know places in Atlanta, Miss Jinx?"

I said a few.

Rune checked his Movado watch. It's easy to tell a Movado watch. Typically their standard pieces have a diamond in the place of the twelve. Rune's was rose gold and at least three grand. Don't ask how I know.

"Meet me at the Georgia Aquarium at eleven tomorrow morning?" Rune asked reaching out to escort me to his office door.

Do I need to tell you that-duh!-I said yes?

So I told Jos and Connie it was all set and they took me back to my office. We made an appointment to meet after the holidays to start looking for venues. I hastily made a reminder for myself to put the appointment in my planner as I released Livia for the day.

Then I went to get Damascus from the day spa. The owner Marie told me that Damascus made a little Yorkie friend named Tomasina. I asked if Tomasina would be in tomorrow and Marie said Tomasina came to doggie daycare every day. So I booked Damascus again for tomorrow and he thanked me by jumping on me. He was definitely getting bigger.

EIGHT

When I got up it was fifty-two degrees. The NBC affiliate weatherman in Atlanta proudly declared that it would be clear, sunny and fifty-six as the high.

"Asshole!" I yelled at him over my room service of fruit cocktail. The room service attendant said there was a Starbuck's two blocks away when I turned away their version of chai tea. So really I had a pre-date with Starbuck's.

It was seven in the morning and I was more nervous about this first date with Rune than I was with Andrea. It might have been more anxiety than anything of what's to come.

But anyway I found a decent pair of jeans in my travel bag and wrinkle-free white sweater with rainbow hearts to put on. It wasn't sexy or anything because it was supposed to be my travel clothes to wear home. The turquoise and lime green Skechers weren't sexy either.

I pulled my straight thick black hair into a high ponytail, applied some Chapstick to my lips and I was ready to go. I mean if I was going to look casual why do makeup?

Damascus and I rode through the Starbuck's for chai tea on our way to the dog

59

spa/daycare. Then we parted ways to give me time to make it the aquarium and park. He was more than happy to get ride of me for the day. He probably didn't want me to mess up any possible flings for him.

So I was standing outside of the massive Georgia Aquarium (basically wrapped around my treinta chai tea) for forty-five minutes. I avoided the crazy look of the other visitors that had the sense to get in line. It might have been because I was obviously freezing.

By the time I started to hunch over against the chill a warm blazer fell on my shoulders.

"Thank you." I forced out, looking for the Good Samaritan.

I found Rune in blue jeans and one of those zip-up sweaters.

"I'm glad I didn't pick the zoo. It's not winter where you come from? Or were you hoping I'd be a gentleman and surrender my coat?" he remarked extending a hand to me.

I took it and he lead the way to the line.

"Honestly Jacksonville only has one cold month...January. But thank you for the loaner." I answered him.

Then I suddenly remembered that he was supposed to tell me how he knew I was a Jinn. So I asked him just as we got to the ticket window.

"Two please." Rune told the attendant, handing the girl his credit card.

The girl smiled, processed the transaction and handed Rune his card and tickets.

"I am too," he uttered squeezing my hand before he got the door for me.

"You are too what? Nervous?" I asked quizzically now inside of the aquarium's huge lobby.

"Possibly. But I was admitting to being a fellow love Jinn. You know...the answer to your question? The prize for going on a date with me?" Rune said softly, escorting me in the direction he wanted to go.

"Seriously?" I asked stopping dead in my tracks.

Rune tugged me forward and when I wouldn't budge he grabbed me around my waist and carted me away.

He set me down right in front of the entrance to the Ocean Voyager. Then he took my hand again after he made sure his blazer was actually on me. He started into the tunnel while a manta ray glided over us.

I was dumbfounded on a few accounts as you can guess.

"I love aquariums. As a Jinn I'll never be a mermaid. But if I could be anything else it would be a mermaid to be under the sea." Rune said softly, standing behind me as I started up at the sea's bounty.

"Come on, Rune. Be serious." I scoffed playfully elbowing him.

"I am serious, Jinx. I wouldn't lie about something like this," he said spinning me around to face him.

I wanted to say something flippant but his gaze was intense. Too intense to be a liar.

Some kids edged around us to press their little faces and hands against the glass.

Rune wasn't going to elaborate in present company. I so wished that we were in a soundproof booth just so he would say something to make me really believe. I mean Grey said there were very few love Jinns in the world. How could I possibly find one six hours away?

"You wished for something, didn't you? I hear the pressure change but I don't see anything." Rune asked eyeing me cautiously.

"You weren't going to talk. You can talk now. No one can hear us." I smiled proudly. I loved knowing I could do magic. However with that same magic I wished away my name from Andrea's mind...Don't think about it!

Rune smiled back both impressed and amused. I was used to that amused look.

"I already told you. I'm a love Jinn. I have been since Aleksander was sixteen." Rune said holding both of my hands.

"Aleksander who? A friend of yours?" I asked loving the feel of my hands in his.

"We were never quite friends; but I am the reason for his many conquests. And he's exactly the reason why I stick to teenagers and young lovers. The older Alek got the bigger ass he became." Rune chuckled easily.

"Hold up! Go back." I stated shaking my head in confusion.

"Back to when?" he asked with an amused grin.

I glared at him as if to say 'the beginning. Duh!'.

"I was born on the coast of Macedonia hence the Greek last name. I've always been different. My mom said she knew I was special (but that's for another date). She named me Rune because it means secret; her little secret. Anyway that was a very long time ago. Like I said when Aleksander was sixteen. We share a birthday." Rune told me, looking up at a carpet shark that had tried to settle on the top of the tunnel.

The kids squealed with apparent delight.

"Aleksander who though?" I insisted ignoring the shark for now. I wanted an answer.

"Aleksander of Macedonia," he stated beginning to move us along.

I've heard that title before. Not only was I a sci-fi/fantasy geek I was a closet history buff.

"Holy shit! Alexander the Great?" I expelled deciding to get rid of the soundproofing now.

"The same. I met him later." Rune laughed at my response.

"That is so cool! Is that where the accent is from?" I beamed. I was holding hands with another love Jinn who was...a *lot* older than me?

Now that was freakin' cool!

"The accent is probably from all of my travels." Rune shrugged and then he suddenly turned to look at me and said:

"So where does a woman as beautiful as you come from?" But he asked in Far'si.

Hold up! "You speak Far'si?"

"It's a language all Jinn know. Plus every other language." Rune laughed again at my response.

OK. Relax Jinx. He's not out to get you.

"I was born and raised in Karaj until I was four. That's in Iran. Then we lived in Cairo for ten years and then we moved to Jackson-ville. So Karaj." I replied in Far'si.

Rune squeezed my hand as a show of understanding.

We continued through the aquarium, chatting and laughing.

"So photography? How does a love Jinn work with photography?" I asked after we sat down to have a late lunch in the aquarium's café.

"It's a way to capture all types of love. That's what you see in my portraits. Love. If I see anything else through my lens I politely refuse the job." Rune said with a sincere smile, stealing a crinkle fry from my plate of fries and kosher slaw dog (I was just in the mood).

"So just weddings and engagement photos?" I pressed, feeling him out. He could be a prospective vendor if nothing else. But I was really hoping Rune would be more than that.

"And newborns. Don't forget the newborns hence the studio in the back. But sometimes I come to the clients' homes to take the pictures. It is a-" Rune smiled.

"Natural progression from weddings." I completed his sentence.

There was that amused look again. But Rune's was mixed with something else...adoration maybe?

"How did you know I was going to say that?" he asked in disbelief.

"I might as well tell you what else I do so you'll understand why I feel the same as you." I sighed looking down at my plate slightly embarrassed. I don't know why. Maybe it wasn't embarrassment but humility?

Rune gestured that I continue while he snacked on his potato chips.

"I started my business Eden after a couple months in community college. I decided to be a matchmaker for people overseas. A guy in my class helped me with the web site and I was off and running, as they say. Matchmaking lead to wedding planning. Wedding planning lead to honeymoon travel agent..." I explained kind of glancing around instead of looking into Rune's blue eyes. Why was I such a dork?

"I'm seeing what you're saying." Rune smiled again causing me to finally look at him.

I melted.

"Two months ago I was in Ireland planning a wedding for some Elfs and the bride to be's sister asked if I could throw her a baby shower. And I did because as I explained to Vi it was natural progression." I said with a little more self-confidence in his eyes. Rune had already heard an earful about Violet.

"And did she agree?" Rune asked probably already knowing that she might not.

"She said next thing you know we'll be doing funerals as a natural progression of things." I pouted.

Rune frowned. "I don't know how much I like Violet. She just went all morbid with that. Obviously she's not a love Jinn. We're talking about the natural progression of pretty things like love."

65

"Yeah. Well she also thinks I'm crazy because I think it would be romantic to die in bed with the man I love. Provided he's dead too." I quipped between sips from my bottled water.

Rune considered that for a few minutes as we headed into a different part of the aquarium.

"Provided you're dead too yes it would be extremely romantic. I wouldn't have to continue on and die of a broken heart nor would you," he said with his arm around my waist.

My heart went thump! And I froze in a good way. Was he just saying that to humor me?

"You must know, Jinx, that what I say to you cannot be a lie. Love Jinns cannot lie to each other or our protectors." Rune added kissing the top of my head.

Where was that written, Grey?

"Have you met another love Jinn before?" I asked meekly.

"A long time ago before they switched sides. I try not to think about it. Maybe I'll tell you at another time. Come see these angry fat otters they have here." Rune answered with a sad look in his eyes for a moment.

By the time Rune had to go get ready for his gig I was hoping he'd skip it for me.

"Would you skip a wedding for me?" Rune asked me seriously.

We were walking out to my car. I wasn't sure if he knew what I was thinking or if he was asking out of his own curiosity.

"Depends. I would love for someone to stand in for me at Mr. Parisi's wedding." I quipped

66

just to be funny. Actually I might have been serious when it came to Mr. Parisi.

"No you wouldn't. But I feel bad for leaving you now after such a great date. You *do* think it was a good date, right?" Rune asked studying my face for some reason.

"Why can't I tag along for your gig?" I wanted to ask but I'm pretty sure I didn't.

"This was an awesome date. But I understand that you have work to do. I had a really great time, Rune." I beamed enthusiastically, standing beside my car. My key fob was in my jeans pocket with my credit card. I left everything else under some random trash in my backseat.

Rune reached around me to push the tiny button on the door handle and unlock the car.

Once the car was unlocked Rune opened the door for me to get behind the wheel. I just moved out of the way and stood there, hopeful. He had to kiss me, right?

Right? We had a connection. There had to be a kiss.

Rune looked from me to the interior and back.

Seriously?

I tried to hide my obvious disappointment as I took the key fob out of my pocket so I didn't sit on it by accident. Then I climbed in and got situated for him to close the door.

"I've got your card. I'll give you a call to go over Jos and Connie's wedding." Rune said oh-so-professionally, starting to close the door.

"I look forward to hearing from you then." I choked out with all of the charm I could muster.

Rune smiled and closed the door finally.

I felt my throat tighten in preparation for a cry when I put my right foot on the brake and pushed the Start button.

What did I do wrong?

Suddenly the door flew open again and Rune yanked me out by the lapels of his blazer I was still wearing.

"Say something." Rune demanded inches from my face.

"Wh-what?" I stammered still so ready to cry out my disappointment.

Rune kissed me gently, waiting on my reaction. Again I melted. I just sighed not fighting what he made me feel.

His mouth opened on mine, easing my mouth open. His tongue didn't cross over. It was just a very deep open mouthed kiss. I could almost see making love to Rune. Wait! Did I just think that?

Rune pulled away and helped me back into my running car. Shit! The car could have been stolen for all I cared while Rune was kissing me.

"I-I still have your coat..." I suddenly recalled again before he could close the door again.

"I'll come get it later. Have a safe trip home." Rune said leaning into my car again to kiss my cheek. Then he shut the door and I watched him walk away.

NINE

Seven days later I was hard at work on Cici and Mr. Parisi's wedding. Cici had one idea for an invitation and Mr. Parisi had another; which was causing a major delay. It also didn't help that my mind wandered.

"Can't we come to some sort of compromise?" Rune asked me exactly a week after I had left Atlanta.

I was taking a Moscato break before I called Cici for an update. I suddenly knew exactly how to push back Mr. Parisi's sidebar commentary. He really wasn't supposed to be interfering with Cici's and my planning anyway.

But while I was working up my nerve Rune had called. We called each other a lot; which was easy because we were in the same time zone.

"Compromise on what?" I said playfully, sitting on my bed with Damascus beside me. I had been in my room when he called, hoping to get a shower in.

"Jinx, come on! You're killing me!" Rune groaned six hours away in Atlanta.

"You act like I'm torturing you." I laughed sipping my wine.

"You are. I want to see you again."

"And again. And again." I added in what I thought was a discrete murmur.

"Exactly!" Rune shouted and I could hear it echo in the back-ground.

I was a little mortified that he heard me; but then I thought of Rune's beautiful blue eyes.

"I have to call a client right now." I said wishing I could see his face.

Just then my phone beeped like there was an incoming call.

I pulled the phone away from my ear to see that I had an incoming Facetime call from Rune. I hit Accept.

"I'm an old man. You can't keep playing with me." Rune remarked right away and I saw his face.

He had a few day old beard with just the right amount of gray in it. My heart stopped. I didn't even think about how sloppy I might have looked with my hair messily on my shoulders.

"You're beautiful..." I whispered in response. Once again I didn't mean for him to hear my sincere reaction to his beauty.

Rune stammered and blushed a little.
"Jinx..."

"You don't look too bad for an old man." I retorted before I could say anything stupid again.

"Jill would tell you that she's never seen me with a beard. And I have a beard because I'm too busy thinking about hearing your voice instead of shaving." Rune huffed looking quite perturbed.

Behind him I could see an apple green wall. I wondered if this was at his home. I hadn't seen inside of his house of course. I just knew he told me he owned a house in eastern Atlanta but still in the city limits.

"You're showering though, right?" I asked pretending to be offended as I got off of my bed. I could see me in the corner of the phone screen and I could also see my black slatted headboard. No need to tempt the man with glimpses of my bedroom.

So I went into the office. Damascus stayed in my room.

Rune glared at me. He didn't find that amusing or charming. His glare though made me laugh and almost drop my wineglass.

"What do you have on your schedule for next week?" Rune asked me when I got my giggles under control.

I opened my planner. Today was Thursday December eleventh. I tapped on the date while Rune paced. Saturday was circled because I was expected in Rock Hill to do Tamara Porter's final fitting (ugh! And florist visits).

After that was Hanukkah which I didn't work (like I said before).

"It can't be that full. Can it?" Rune remarked finally.

"Saturday I'm in Rock Hill, South Carolina all day; if not all weekend. Then I'm off from the start of Hanukkah on Tuesday for a week. After that I have to be in Portugal; which brings me back to the need to call my client." I reported from the planner.

Rune repeated back my schedule.

"I have a Christmas Eve reception on my calendar and a newborn thing on this coming Monday. Did you say Hanukkah?" he said next.

I nodded. "I grew up between a few worlds: Islamic and Jewish."

"So you have a lot of holidays, huh?" Rune grinned with his genuine accent.

"I celebrate a few...Passover, Ramadan and Hanukkah..." I smiled timidly.

"We might have a few of those in common. I'm Greek Orthodox. I don't celebrate Christmas." Rune admitted.

No. No Christmas but he would celebrate Three Kings Day in January. Either way neither one of us would be shopping for a Christmas tree in our futures.

"Call your client and I'll call you back later. Maybe I can find a razor around here to shave." Rune said with a wink. I could see the wheels behind his eyes churning. He was about to plan something.

"I like the beard. Keep it just a little longer." I said softly, awkwardly. I was such a dork!

"Only because you said so. I'll call you in about an hour," he grinned, ending our Facetime session.

I hurriedly dialed up Cici. I told her that we were going to order her choice of invitations despite Mr. Parisi's little tantrums.

"When it's all said and done, Cici, he's going to be too amazed to complain." I added to Cici as I submitted the rush invitation order.

When I received the confirmation email I forwarded it to Cici's email address, printed a copy for the file and saved it in my business email.

"I really think you're going to be right about that, Jinx. I'll let you know when I have mailed out the invitations." Cici responded sounding optimistic.

"I'll call you before then. Hopefully on Tuesday. We have a Skype appointment with a fabulous dressmaker I found online. He has a whole bunch of ready-made dresses that he said you could come in and try. Remember?" I replied seeing the appointment pop up to flash at me. I quickly wrote the appointment in my planner because it wasn't there already.

"I have the reminder and address on my phone. I'll be there. Til Tuesday then. Ciao." Cici said ending the call.

Then I ran to take that shower and refill my wineglass before Rune could Facetime or call me back.

By the time Rune did Facetime I was curled up on the loveseat watching a re-air of this week's Doctor Who. Damascus was asleep on his little bed in my room.

"I've got a plan. Are you ready to hear it?" Rune said right away.

We both appeared to be ready for bed. I wore my hair up for bed so I didn't strangle myself or lay on it (my mother's mother used to have some story behind the principle. But Mene was a little crazy). Rune pulled his hair back with an elastic headband. His hair wasn't as long as

Andrea's but it was full and to the bottom of his neck. It was kinda sexy in a weird way.

"I'm all ears!" I exclaimed turning off the TV.

"We're going to spend next weekend in Charleston. I've booked us at a resort I've done a wedding at before. I've always wanted to go back and enjoy it with someone. Who better than a woman I care for?" Rune smiled and looked completely excited about the adventure.

"Is that your way of saying...what?" I asked suddenly falling flat. I even looked at my half empty wineglass to ask why the sudden mood swing.

"My way of saying I want to spend time with you. What's wrong, Jinx?" he said and his smile slowly faded.

"I...I'm scared..." I whispered more to the wineglass than to Rune.

"Too soon?" Rune asked with concern. I had told him about Andrea a couple days ago. He was very sweet about it and said he didn't want to push me if I wasn't ready.

Was it too soon? I mean what if Rune was really perfect for me and I brushed him off to wait a gazillion years for the possibility of Andrea?

"Rune, what do you know about the love lives of love Jinn?" I asked to somewhat calm my nerves.

"It depends. We're not supposed to marry. That's constant because we are supposed to serve others. But it's been pretty easy for us also. Ninety percent of love Jinn are males you know. Even with lesser numbers there's still only male love Jinns. The females always give in and go the way of the wind." Rune explained.

"Because women think more with our hearts." I added. It's true and I'm cool with that.

"Which also makes them stronger than men. So if they switch sides that's a very formidable Jinn. But the love Jinns do fall in love and lead lives that allow them to settle into society. I just always moved. I've never found anyone worth all of my time before..." Rune concluded with a sigh. An actual sigh.

"You think you found that someone now?" I asked shyly, beginning to feel a blush come on.

"Jinx...I really want to find out. I know I said I wouldn't push the issue...And I don't even know if we can be together for real...I just have to know." Rune said like he was truly in some despair over us.

"Usually if I'm about to do something illegal in the Jinn world Grey shows up to stop me." I told him with a telling smile. I even looked around in case Grey was lurking somewhere in the shadows of my house.

Rune burst out laughing. "Conrad would be here in an instant protesting in his whiny Greek voice."

Conrad must have been Rune's protector.

When he was done laughing I knew my answer. I was really into Rune. He was (dare I say) hotter than Andrea. He was so cool and I couldn't wait to learn more about him. Don't tell Andrea I said that.

"Let's do it!" I exclaimed emphatically.

"Really? You'll go with me to Charleston?" Rune beamed perking up a lot.

"Yes. I'd be stupid not to." I laughed or more like giggled.

Rune was completely relieved now so he could finally go to bed.

I, on the other hand, was up for another hour staring at my bedroom ceiling. I couldn't stop fantasizing about lying next to Rune next week. But finally I passed out still fantasizing (so I woke up in a puddle of my own drool).

TEN

OK...So I finally got to Thursday, the second full day of Hanukkah. No lie! I woke up to a call from Rune who was on his way to the airport. His flight was earlier than mine so he could meet me at the airport. My flight was....

"Holy shit! I've got to get going, babe! I'll call you from the airport before I leave!"

Did I just call him babe?

That was how soon my flight was. Thankfully I had dropped Damascus off with Grey last night (I knew Grey but he asked what I wanted for Christmas even though I don't celebrate and I told him a week of dog-sitting. And seriously he said bring Damascus over).

So I still had to hurry but Rune understood.

Forty minutes later I was backing out of the garage with three bags full of everything I might possibly need. I couldn't decided if it would be consistently warm or cold in Charleston so I packed a little of everything.

I closed the garage door, honked at Mr. Michael next door putting up Christmas lights and headed to the airport.

Then I was off to Jacksonville International Airport so psyched I think I was even more excited to go on this trip to see Rune in Charleston than I was to see Andrea in Italy. Maybe it was because of the banter between us where Andrea and I didn't have a lot of meaningless chatter (Rune and I did but it was fun).

I was pondering this when my iPhone rang on the charger tucked behind the shifter. I pulled it out, slide the screen to the right to answer the call. Then I hit Speaker so I could partially concentrate on driving.

Besides my mind was whirling with new fantasies of me and Rune.

"Oh my God! I've been such an idiot!" Violet shouted immediately. Good ole' Vi! All about her...sometimes.

"Happy Hanukkah, Jinx! How are you? Why, thank you, Vi. Funny you should ask..." I said in response dramatically.

"Oh whatever, Jinxie. There's six days of it. In the meantime I have a major issue." Vi remarked ignoring my sarcasm.

"What's your major issue?" I sighed almost grateful that we weren't talking about me.

I made the mistake (maybe) of telling Violet about Andrea two days or so into meeting him. This time I was going to wait maybe a few months. I never had any etiquette about this when to tell your family and friends about the love of your life. Anyone have any pointers?

"Did you hear me? I was reading the little notes wrong!" Violet shouted breaking my little mental ramble.

I wanted to ask what notes but then…duh…I remembered. We're talking about Kyle.

"What did you get wrong? He didn't mean to send them to you?" I quipped taking my exit to I-95 North.

I was really driving as fast as I could. My flight left in an hour and a half. And if I was lucky pedestrian traffic would be light on a Thursday early afternoon and I wouldn't hit anyone…Who was I kidding?

"Very funny, Jinx. The numbers weren't GPS coordinates! It's a countdown!" Violet expelled sounding a little panicked.

Countdown?

ELEVEN

Countdown?" I replied thinking of all sorts of crazy things now.

Who sends someone a countdown? Kyle that's who. He was probably an undercover terrorist. He was going to probably bomb Skylar and Violet's flat in a jealous rage. He looked like the sort.

"I hate when you do that." Violet groaned interrupting me again.

"It's an unconscious thing. What's up with the countdown?" I said focusing on what she was saying. Even though I wouldn't care less about Kyle and his goings-on.

"It's a countdown until he'll be here. He's using Greenwich time," she squealed.

"How did you figure this out? And I don't like how you just said 'until he'll be here'. Sounds like the apocalypse." I remarked flatly, getting off on the Airport exit where the actual airport sat at the very end past the River City Town Center (the second outdoor shopping mall like the St. Johns Town Center just smaller).

Almost there!

"Skylar did. I accidentally left one of the notes out and he stared at it for a second. Then he asked me why I had Greenwich times written down." Violet gushed.

So that Skylar thing definitely wasn't a romantic relationship if he just casually asked this. I don't know if I felt bad for Skylar or not.

"So what time is Kyle actually supposed to be there?" I asked trying to get to the point of the call. Personally I wanted to get back to daydreaming about Rune.

"I actually don't know. Skylar said that the time and date were all in Zulu time. And I'm at work now and the notes are at home. I just had to tell you how stupid I was." Violet concluded which I was grateful. I had enough anxiety without listening to Violet's drama.

"OK. Good to know. Let me know what you find out. You know in case I need to testify in court to his evil deeds." I replied briskly breezing through a few yellow lights.

"You're so funny, Jinx. I'll let you know what I find out." Violet laughed ending the call.

I pulled the phone off of the charger, dropped the phone into my smaller Michael Kors purse and took the charger.

Needless to say I was doing the fastest walk possible to the terminal after getting through the TSA checkpoint. I was going to run but I didn't want to sweat in my new red sweater dress that I ordered online last week.

But I made it to my flight and into Charleston. I've never been to Charleston. I thought of horse-drawn carriages and Rhett Butler when I heard the word Charleston (my Mene was

81

a big Gone With the Wind fan. Like I said she was crazy). With that said I was excited to be here.

I stepped out of the terminal to head to the baggage claim and I was immediately snatched up into a man's arms. I wanted to panic because I've been abducted twice in less than six months (basically I'm skittish).

"Surprise!" Rune exclaimed spinning me around before he put me down.

"You scared me!" I expelled playfully, slapping his arm.

He stepped back to take me in and he looked really appreciative. I was really appreciative too seeing how his cream cable knit sweater laid on him. Wow!

"I wasn't sure if it was going to be warm or cold here. I brought back your blazer too." I said nervously as we plucked my Jansport luggage off of the conveyor belt.

"You didn't..." Rune said eyeing me seriously.

"I didn't what? Bring back the blazer? Yeah. You said the next time you saw me...Didn't you?" I uttered stopping in my tracks.

Rune took out his phone to snap a picture of me.

"I said I would come get it. Until then I don't want it. Come on! My bags are in the trunk. I rented a pretty Mustang for the weekend. You're going to love this place...I hope." Rune beamed putting his phone away to help me with my bags.

Then we left the airport and drove to The Sanctuary Hotel on Kiawah Island.

It was freakin' gorgeous! And our room overlooked the pool and ocean! I had never been this spellbound about a place but I would definitely recommend Kiawah Island for a destination wedding or honeymoon.

"You're always thinking about work, aren't you?" Rune asked, watching me put a business card from the hotel manager into my purse.

"Never know." I shrugged timidly, starting on unpacking.

Rune unpacked too and then we stood there looking at each other. I was looking at him on the sly while I perused the room service menu.

"Would you like to go down to the bar? We can have a drink before dinner…" Rune suggested optimistically.

"Absolutely! Should we eat here or go into Charleston?" I beamed putting the menu away.

"Let's have a drink first." Rune smiled back extending his hands to me.

I took them and slid off the king bed.

We went downstairs to the bar and had two drinks each while Rune asked the bartender for the local hangouts. Rune was very good at engaging people and I loved watching him work.

"What do you two do for a living?" the bartender Phil asked us after two hours of chatting.

"I'm a wedding planner/matchmaker. He's a photographer." I answered over my wineglass.

Phil looked impressed. "If you really want to have a good time go to Closed for Business or Blind Tiger Pub. I used to work at the Blind Tiger part time when I started college. It pays better here though."

"So the Blind Tiger Pub and Closed for Business? We'll try them out. Thanks Phil." Rune smiled finishing his glass of beer.

Then we went back up to our room to change and head into town. I took a risk and put on a short black halter dress that I wore a few weeks ago to a Halloween party with Grey (we were supposed to be Bonnie and Clyde or something). The dress hugged me closer than Rune.

"That dress and I are going to have issues." Rune remarked from the bathroom where he was trimming his beard.

I always got ready quickly so I was attempting to pace unnoticed around the bed. I was nervous as hell.

Rune could catch glimpses of me (I suppose) in the bathroom mirror so he knew what I was wearing. I didn't peek at what he was wearing. My heart was pounding in anticipation.

"Think it'll be too hard to get off?" I teased trying to fuss with my hair now. I had it down with a thin black jeweled headband but maybe it should have been up?

Rune came out of the bathroom and slipped up behind me. He grabbed up all of my hair in one hand, placed the other hand on my right hip and kissed the back of my neck. The shiver that ran down my body made me hot (I wasn't wearing a bra and that was probably evident now).

"Jinx, I am so glad I waited on you," he whispered over the skin on my neck.

I was literally putty in his hands. Whatever Rune wanted he could have.

"Rune..." I whispered back with my eyes closed and my head back on his shoulder.

He kissed my neck again briskly and pinned up my hair quickly.

"It goes up. It goes down later," he stated moving away from me.

I opened my eyes to spy my black hair in a messy knot held in place with the clip I tied my hair back with for showers. Cute!

I pivoted around to check out Rune. My heart stopped and I stumbled back into the dresser I was standing in front of.

Rune was adjusting the cuffs of his long sleeved slate gray collared shirt so he didn't see my misstep. He was also wearing black fitted pants over black Cole Haans. His brown hair was slicked down with hair gel.

When he looked up at me with those blue eyes I was actually crying (WTF?).

"Are you OK?" Rune asked starting to come closer to me. But he stopped and smiled like he knew why I was crying.

"I'm being silly..." I uttered wiping away the tears with my fingertips.

"I'm just an ordinary man, Jinx. Nothing extra special here," he said humbly, coming towards me again.

"You're extra special alright. You'd have to be. You're a Jinn." I laughed off his humility.

"Then we'll be an extraordinary couple. Let me get us out of here before we can't." Rune grinned, running his hands down my bare arms.

"Are we going to make it to the bar?" I asked flirtatiously, tugging on the hem of my dress after I got in the car.

"Maybe…" Rune grinned shifting the car into gear.

We did. We went to Closed for Business first and kinda stayed there.

Rune ordered my drinks so I tried different things. I was determined to stick with my wine but Rune wasn't having it.

I trusted him even after five Captains and Coke.

I was on the sixth one when I noticed I was fucked up (not messed up…fucked up).

My hands kept finding their way into Rune's pants or his shirt or his hair. And his hands travelled freely over my body headily but respectfully unlike me. His mouth kept calling me so I was on it constantly.

"Jinx, we're not going to make it back to the hotel," he told me as his lips kissed my ear for the fourth time.

"Too drunk?" I giggled wrapping my arms around his neck lazily. I remembered doing the same move with Andrea but the man in front of me was completely different from Andrea. Rune was the epitome of sexy. I concede that now and always.

"No, I'm doing alright to drive. I was referring to how I am feeling about you." Rune said pulling away to look me in the eyes. He was sitting on a bar stool and I was standing between his legs dancing.

I pouted. "But I don't want to fuck in the car our first time."

"We're not going to fuck anyway." Rune remarked leaning back against the bar to take a drink from his glass of Uzo. He was obviously a Greek through and through. He had asked for a liquor called Tsipouro but they didn't have it.

My mouth dropped open to protest. He quickly placed his mouth over it. I melted again and I closed my eyes to lose myself in his embrace.

Rune released me, finished his drink and took me by the hand to lead me out of the bar.

We walked back to the car and Rune rested me against it. I leaned into him, kissing his neck and shoulders.

"Did you make love to him?" Rune asked seriously with his hands on the roof of the car, corralling me between his arms.

I stopped kissing him, hearing something like pain or jealousy in his voice. Was he wanting the truth? Because he was going to get it drunk or not ('it' could be sex or truth at this point).

"Rune..." I answered feeling my high fall.

"If you made love to him, then why would you fuck me?" he asked, lifting my chin to look up at him in the darkness.

I was drunk and thoroughly confused by Rune's question. I must have looked it too because Rune added to his statement.

"Do you think less of me than you did of Andrea?"

Oh! I get it now!

"Rune, I think that you and i have a different connection. Completely different connection." I responded sincerely, considering all our conversations, all of our meaningless chatter, all of our playful banter.

"Truer? Did you make out with him when you were drunk?" he asked next, putting his hands on my hips now.

Was this becoming a competition? Rune against Andrea? Jinn versus gargoyle? Ugh!

"Rune, I was barely with Andrea before I let him marry a gargoyle princess." I huffed crossing my arms over my chest to show my displeasure with this competition.

Rune eyed me suspiciously, but once again knowing I was speaking the truth.

"Will you fuck me?" he asked with a grin itching at the corners of his mouth.

"Oh! You're going to get fucked alright." I growled kissing him hard on the mouth and igniting that fire that had been there.

Thirty minutes later I lead him to the bed after kicking off my stacked sandals at the door. I pulled him close (with what I hoped was a dangerous look) to unbutton his shirt. He stood there running his hands up and down my arms anxiously.

When I got the shirt unbuttoned to reveal the shadow of a six pack on a flat stomach Rune spun me around to kiss the back of my neck. He undid the tie around my neck and shimmied the rest of the dress down my body. Lastly he undid my hair just like he said would happen.

Rune turned me back around to kiss me deeply. I fell into him, for him and with him.

TWELVE

He laid me down on the bed like I was the most precious thing on Earth while he kissed all over my body.

Then just before I thought he was going to finally make love to me he stopped to look down at me.

"I should tell you two things that Conrad told me before I left Atlanta..."

"So Conrad knows that you're here with me?" I asked flatly, looking up at him still quite buzzed.

He nodded and quickly said what he needed to say.

"I can't get you pregnant unless you wish (of course). And this is supposed to be spectacular. I don't know about the last part..."

"Great. Shut up and let me make that decision." I remarked sitting up to kiss him again.

And that did shut him up for a while. I'm the one that couldn't shut up and Rune seemed to enjoy that.

I can tell you that an hour flew by in forty-five minutes.

When Rune clambered off the bed to get something that was the first time I saw what he was working with. I mean I felt it and everything at the bar; but it didn't really prepare me for reality.

He wasn't built like Andrea or anything (which made Rune far more enjoyable).

Rune pulled something out of his travel bag that struck me odd – a bottle of wine. Then he pulled out his camera and I immediately headed for the covers.

"Are you crazy?" I blurted out staring in horror at the camera like Rune had just pulled Satan out of his bags.

"Not that I know of. This wine's too much? I though we would celebrate our first evening together. I can put it on ice for later or not?" Rune responded pausing with the cork opener.

"What about the camera?" I asked with the white duvet up to my chin. My parents would kill somebody if they found naked photos of me somewhere, anywhere. Shit! I don't even have naked baby pictures if that says anything (it does. I'm Muslim and Jewish and they don't play that game).

Rune looked at me and then his camera on the little table next to him and back.

"You're so funny!" Rune burst out laughing but continued with de-corking the wine.

"You're not using that now?" I asked feeling a little more confident.

"Jinx, we'd have to know each other a while before I took those kind of photos of you." Rune told me, pouring the wine into two plastic cups that came with the room.

He brought one to me and then got back into bed with me, holding the other.

"Did Conrad object to you seeing me?" I asked to change the subject. I took a sip of wine to find that I wasn't buzzed anymore (but I was thirsty as hell).

"Not at all. He said that we might be in for a pleasant surprise. He said that it had been ages since two love Jinn or Jinn had dated…" Rune replied looking away from me suddenly. He sipped his wine but I read something else into his statement.

"He said it had been ages since *you* had been with another Jinn to be exact. Didn't he? You have pension for other Jinns?" I said astutely, less confident. Man! I was going through it with him.

"I don't have a pension for other Jinns. I was young and had a thing for older women. She just happened to be a love Jinn. It didn't last long. She fell in love with a mortal and crossed over to a Jinn of fortune." Rune explained curtly, drinking his wine.

I nodded, waiting him out.

"Conrad said you wouldn't be like that. I made him swear. A protector's promise is even more binding than one of our wishes." Rune added darkly, putting his cup down to gaze back at me.

He was so beautiful. More beautiful than any man on Earth. Well at least to me even with that crooked tooth. I can't explain my sudden change of heart from Andrea to Rune. I just knew that with Rune I could possibly be me if I gave it half a chance.

"We'll go slow…" we both said at the same time.

I laughed because I couldn't believe we were thinking the same thing.

Rune kissed me, bringing me back down onto the mattress where he found his way inside of me again.

The next morning I woke up in his arms with him purring away in my hair. He was exhausted so I let him snore softly, lying there so content.

Or at least I thought he was asleep.

"You're awake, aren't you?" Rune suddenly asked while I was re-living last night, this morning.

"Go back to sleep." I hissed stroking his chest.

"Can't. I have a tee time set up for us this morning." Rune yawned and then kissed the top of my head.

I was going to ask if he was joking but something about how he said it let me know he was serious.

"I don't know how to golf, baby." I huffed sitting up to gawk down at him.

"You're going to learn. I bet you get it right on the first tee," he smiled lazily, sitting up on the backs of his forearms.

"You aren't secretly wishing that I'm a golf prodigy, are you?" I asked him suspiciously, holding back my smile. I couldn't help but to smile when he did.

"Now that would just be cheating. Besides I can't make you do anything against your will. Hence you have to want a baby to get pregnant," he grinned tilting his head to kiss my back. His beard tickled me and turned me on.

I considered that (what he had said) while he called dibs on the bathroom. I could almost see myself slipping up in the future and wishing a baby for Rune. This was new for me. I never thought that way about Andrea. I never really saw a future like that for us.

Anyway Rune came out of the bathroom without a beard and in white shorts and a turquoise golf shirt. He was holding his golf shoes in his hands, gesturing that I was next.

But when I came out in my bra and undies Rune had my little golf outfit set out on the messy bed. He had this planned literally to the tee right down to the right sized shoes and socks.

"How did you do that?" I gasped as I put on the clothes.

"Uh…I wished it, babe. I'm a Jinn." Rune said wryly, leaning against the dresser. He was completely dressed watching me.

"Just say 'duh, you idiot'." I quipped slapping his left arm after I popped my head through my white polo shirt.

"No. It's fun seeing your reaction," he laughed.

So then he wished for a set of golf clubs and off we went for our morning tee time. Well after a croissant and a chai tea. Rune knew my day didn't start without my tea. So it was tea and then tee.

We got a cart and a map and started our golf date.

Four hours later and six holes we gave up because we were going to die laughing if we continued. We laughed at each other, other golfers and old awkward moments. I was to tears laughing so we gave up on golf and got ready for another night in Charleston.

And every day of my little holiday weekend with Rune was fantastic. Really fantastic!

"I don't want to let you go, Jinx?" Rune said sincerely, holding my hand as we walked on the resort's beach Sunday night.

This sounded familiar. I was distraught at leaving Andrea after a few days and wished that he would always love me, never leave me.

"So what would you like to do?" I asked instead sounding hopeful. Somehow I just knew I didn't need to wish Rune felt that way about me.

"Well we can keep this going, right?" Rune asked optimistically, bringing my hand to his mouth to kiss.

"I sure hope so. Can I ask something?" I asked feeling stupid about what I was going to ask. It was against all of the rules and tips (and I'll probably admit in this week's blog) but I just had to know.

"You're my girl. I'll be here when you get back from Portugal or wherever it is that you go." Rune said before I could ask.

"And you're fine with being mine?" I asked stopping to look up at beautiful Rune.

"I don't want to belong to any other female, woman or Jinn. I'm excited that we've laid claim on each other," he smiled pulling me into his arms where I stayed for a while.

"How do you feel about dogs?" I asked casually.

THIRTEEN

Two weeks later I was dressed in a beige floral sundress fussing about where the floral bouquets should go with Cici's adult daughter Lara.

"They're only so big, Lara. They need to go in the middle of each table. Michel had them placed there specifically." I said calmly in Portuguese.

Lara kept taking the floral table settings and removing them from their designated spots. She'd move them to one spot and then move them back. And it was beginning to drive me crazy because I couldn't leave her alone in the reception room to check on Cici or Adolfo without worrying.

"But they would look so good over here...or over there." Lara muttered, hurrying back and forth with two table toppers in her hands.

"Lara? What are you doing in here? Your mom is looking for you for pictures," a young man said in some sort of exasperation.

Then he caught sight of me trying to barricade Lara from a table. If I could save just one table I would know how to fix the others.

"I apologize for my wife. She's very OCD. Once she's fixated on something...look out," the young man said sincerely, taking the table toppers from Lara's hands.

"Don't worry. I'll have her take her medication and she will be right as rain," he added with a smile.

I flashed an understanding smile and waited for them to leave.

The second the door closed I began running around the room fixing the table toppers. The wedding was to begin out by the beach and I still had to make sure everything was on point.

So once I was done with that I hightailed it out of the resort's main building to the ceremony site. I was just in the nick of time because Mr. Parisi (Adolfo) was just coming out with his four sons. He spied me making the corner for the beach I was sure; but he didn't say anything when I greeted him at the end of the walk.

I escorted them to where they should stand just like in last night's rehearsal and then I went to go wait for Cici.

Fifteen minutes later everything was going like clockwork. The resort photographer patiently took pictures before the new Mr. and Mrs. Parisi arrived at the reception of beige and teal in one of the resort's banquet rooms. I had ran ahead to make sure the buffet was set out and no table toppers had moved.

In an old reality (the one where Violet was my part-time assistant) I would show up at the reception with the newlyweds. Violet would have gone on ahead to the reception site to prep and maintain. But in this reality I ran around like a chicken with its head cut off as Southerners say (I don't understand the term literally but I get the gist).

When Adolfo and Cici opened the banquet room doors there were cheers and applause. I stood there with champagne flutes of sparkling wine as planned. They took their flutes, raised them in toast to their guests and took a first sip. Then I escorted them to the larger table in the center of the room away from the dance floor and jazz band.

After they were seated I milled about gauging everyone's satisfaction with the affair. Some guests took my business card. Some asked for advice. Some noticed my phone kept ringing.

After the fifth person recognizing my phone ring I stepped out into the hall to check my messages.

"Hey, it's me. You were on my mind. I posted some of our vacation photos finally. You're so beautiful you know that? I can't wait to see you again."

I didn't even finish listening to the message. I just hit Call Back.

Rune answered right away.

"I didn't mean to take you away from your work. I just wanted to hear your voice on the voice mail."

"It wasn't enough to hear yours on my voice mail. I know it's stupid, lame, ew...gross." I replied trying to make a joke at the end.

"I don't think it is. I only have a moment while the parents dress the baby. Do you think I can call later? What time is it there?" Rune asked probably smiling.

"It's almost six here. You're doing a shooting on New Year's Eve?" I responded, imagining a baby wearing some sparkly headband that looked like fireworks.

"And you're doing a wedding on New Year's. We both should be together at midnight." Rune remarked.

"Nah! Midnight's nothing. In my family it's always more important to be with who you love on New Year's Day. I'm not sure where that notion came from but I'm sure there's a story somewhere." I said offhandedly, opening my Expedia app to confirm my outgoing flight. I was supposed to leave Portugal at nine tonight and land in Atlanta tomorrow (Rune didn't know that).

"Well then I'll give you a call the moment I wake up in the New Year. Does that sound good?" Rune said encouragingly, probably getting back to work.

I said that sounded fantastic, ending the call.

I made a move to go back into the reception only to come face to face with Mr. Parisi. Apparently he had snuck up on me.

"You have done very well, Miss Jinx." Mr. Parisi stated gruffly, extending an envelope to me with my name on it. My one percent fee (that's my take-home pay).

"Thank you, Mr. Parisi. It has been a pleasure to find your wife and see it through fruition." I smiled earnestly, accepting the envelope.

"You are a good young lady. Always gave me much respect even though I am an old ass.

Your parents have been much blessed with you. The young man to whom you speak is also indeed fortunate. One of my sons was quite taken with you but you are too good for him. However I will send him to your site so don't be alarmed when you see the name Parisi again, my dear." Mr. Parisi embellished, bowing to me and then kissing both of my cheeks.

I returned the gesture and Mr. Parisi went back inside. I went back to my room to change into travel-worthy, freezing-Atlanta-worthy clothes. I zipped up my bags and took them and my room key back downstairs with me. I checked out and checked in on the reception one last time.

Michel, the events coordinator, was there overseeing too. I told him to make sure the Parisis had the best time at the resort; especially Mr. Parisi. Michel gave me a brief salute and I was off to the Lisbon airport.

It was a direct flight; which was rare and costly, but I felt it was so worth it. I got off the flight in Atlanta at five in the morning, got into my already-ready-for-me rental Subaru and drove to Rune's townhouse. Technically I was exhausted (and as a Jinn I probably couldn't have gotten to Rune without spending a dime) but I got there, parked on the street behind his neighbor's two door Altima (making me a tad envious) and trotted up the stairs to the door.

I rang the doorbell and waited.

Three minutes later I hear Rune saying 'who is it' and flicking on the porchlight.

"It's me!" I called back softly so I didn't disturb anyone else.

"It can't be..." Rune muttered in Greek on the other side of the door.

He undid the locks and pried open the door, slowly just in case. Then his face lit up.

"Baby! How...what...shit!" Rune exclaimed swinging open the door to grab me into his arms. Something metallic hit the floor behind Rune as he did this. It sounded like a sword.

It *was* a sword just like Grey's except it was black metal.

"What's with the sword? Thought I was another immortal out for your head or something?" I quipped making some reference to-

"Highlander? Really, Jinx? The sword is for protection. I was having some bad feelings when I went to sleep last night. And then I was awoken by an angel," he quipped back catching my drift which was awesome.

"So a sword was going to be helpful?" I asked wide-eyed as he closed the front door.

Rune picked up the sword deftly with one hand, examining it for any faults. He looked at me and then handed it to me by the hilt which wasn't separate from the sword. It was all one piece.

"Lover not a fighter." I stated putting my hands up in a gesture of no harm.

"It's a matter of defense..." Rune said with a serious face.

I was really too tired to argue about it with him. My eyes darted to his mahogany staircase and back to him.

101

"Who am I kidding? This is Conrad's sword. Good thing he doesn't know I just wished it off his person wherever he is." Rune laughed tossing the sword in the air where it disappeared. Presumably it went back to Conrad.

Then Rune swept me up into his arms to carry up to his bed. I had been here before the night I flew to Portugal so I did know what his bedroom looked like. It wasn't the green apple green; that was his living room.

He laid me in the bed with my clothes on and I took one sniff of Rune's soap and passed out.

FOURTEEN

Can I have you look at something and give me
your honest opinion?" Rune asked me two days
later.

I had been fully rested and fully satisfied
for two days. Now we were in his studio before he
closed for Three Kings Day.

Before you say anything Damascus was at
home with Grey and I had checked in on them
both. Apparently Grey was trying to teach
Damascus things that would protect me in the
event Grey wasn't there. I was kind of afraid to
find out what that meant. But my next trip I was
going to bring Damascus along...somehow...

"Sure!" I piped cheerfully, taking his hand
to be led into the dark room.

Negatives hung on lines under the red
light dripping into pans of solvent. The scene
reminded me of an Audrey Hepburn film Funny
Face when she hides in the dark room to see her
face everywhere. And my face was in some of the
developing prints.

But Rune didn't want me to look at that.
Instead he led me to a series of pictures he took
while I was gone.

"I took these with my new camera. These were engagement photos," he told me as he took a print from a line.

It looked like an Asian girl with a light-haired white guy. They made a pretty picture; but something was off.

"Why is that they "were" engagement photos?" I asked using air quotations and whispering.

"I can't possibly charge this couple for these. They're not right." Rune sighed sadly. "So you see what I see?"

"Maybe you can ask that they do another sitting free of charge? It's about customer referrals." I suggested optimistically, taking the print delicately in my fingertips to study farther.

Rune's normal portraits breathed life, harmony, love. This print in my hands felt darkly off. I didn't see anything sweet or loving about the print. It felt devoid of life, silent.

"I've used the camera six times on different clients and you. Every picture looks like that one except for yours." Rune explained taking the print back to hang up.

I moved to look at my pictures and I looked great. I could hear my laughter looking at the picture he took of me at the fort. We had been teasing each other with ghost stories when Rune took the shot. My ghost stories were make-believe, I wasn't sure if Rune's were though.

"That's weird then because they should all look the same, right?" I remarked glancing over at troubled Rune's face.

He was truly upset about this. The camera had probably cost a fortune on top of the possibility of losing business.

Rune nodded turning his frown upside down. "Come on. Let's go celebrate Three Kings. We'll figure this out later."

But we didn't.

I flew home the next night and hugged and kissed on Damascus for a while. Grey wasn't there thankfully so I didn't know what my puppy had learned. Then Damascus and I vegged out on a Hobbit marathon the next day. I should've been working but as the boss I could do what I wanted.

So I went back to work on the eighth; which was a Thursday to sort through a ton of emails. Before I took that week off for Hanukkah I was working on eleven weddings. I was done with one (Mr. Parisi's) but I had ten more to go...maybe it was twelve weddings with eleven to go?

"Have you ever been to Crete, Miss Jinx?" Nora Post-Atkins was asking me when it dawned on me that I hadn't heard from Rune since Monday afternoon.

"I've been to Cyprus on holiday once." I answered lacking my previous enthusiasm. I really had been to Cyprus on a family holiday when I was eight. It was beautiful.

However...had it really been two days since I had talked to Rune? How was that possible? We talked fifty times a day especially at night.

"Cyprus? Can Brits go there? We hadn't thought of Cyprus. Dave, did you know about

Cyprus?" Nora responded speaking to me and her fiancé David Cowell (you know like Simon Cowell...but not, was how David introduced himself).

Two whole days and not a word, I kept thinking. Ok Jinx. Work first, worry later.

I flipped back on the enthusiasm switch to puzzle out a destination site for this destination wedding. Nora and David wanted to check out these sites firsthand before they chose a spot. So with that in mind I told them I would do some research and get back with them to set something up.

Nora said OK and I closed the office for the evening.

I walked Damascus after dinner with my phone in my pocket in case I had been missing Rune's calls. But no calls came through. We came back to the house and I took a shower. Still no calls.

After my shower I poured a glass of wine, turned out all of the lights and locked up.

"Movie night again, Damascus. New episodes of Doctor Who don't start until next week." I said to Damascus as I stood in front of the DVD bookcase with the glass of Moscato in my hand. Damascus went for the couch on cue.

I decided to watch 300 because it was Greek (except for Gerard Butler with his Scottish brogue). It was Greek and semi-romantic. Basically all it did was make me think of Rune.

Gerard, Damascus and I didn't last long.

I couldn't stop thinking about Rune; especially during that first sex scene. I made it about ten more minutes and turned the DVD and TV off. I trudged into my bedroom (that I hadn't shared with Rune yet), fell into my bed and tried to sleep.

I woke up an hour later at the beginning of a winter rainfall in a cold sweat. Something was bothering me...namely no communication with Rune. I just kept thinking about him. Where was he? What was he doing?

What *was* he doing? Was I just a fling? Was he fucking the shit out of some other girl now? Was he sleeping with Jill? OMG!! Was he in bed with Jill right now?

I fumbled on my night table for my iPhone to call him. I found it, searched recent calls and dialed Rune on speaker.

Ring! Ring! Ring!

"Good day! You've reached Kalakos Photography. I'm away from my phone. Please leave a message and I will call you back within twenty-four hours. Thank you for your business."

Beep!

"Hey baby! It's me. I haven't heard from you in a few days. I just wanted to make sure everything's OK...You're on my mind. Call me." I said into his voice mail. Then I hung up.

Simmer down, Jinxie. He's not fucking someone else. He's just busy, my conscience tried to calm me so I could sleep.

Busy doing what at midnight? He'd answer before, I told myself.

I wasn't going to be sleeping anytime soon.

I didn't sleep. I stayed in bed until four in the morning. Then I got up quietly so I didn't disturb Damascus and started my office Keurig with some chai tea. Might as well work, right?

Around one after I did my blog and walked Damascus I tried Rune again. Normally we talked first thing, then at two and six and then at bedtime. Calling at one would be my test if he hadn't ditched me for some other chick (the word I really wanted to use was the b word).

The phone rang once and then I was sent to voice mail.

I immediately hung up, put my phone down carefully so I didn't break it and broke down in tears.

FIFTEEN

I cried off and on until Grey showed up on Wednesday to dog-sit. Damascus and Grey must have known something I forgot because Damascus stood by the front door waiting on Grey.

"Are you packed and ready? Why do you look like you've been ran over by a Mack truck?" Grey asked heading into Violet's old room with his bag of clothes and stuff.

"Do I really look that bad? Why are you here?" I asked in response, closing the front door after my guest and protector.

Grey had an arrogance about him. He has saved me a few times in the past few months. But he's still an asshole; a very pretty one.

"You look like you haven't slept in days. I'm here because you're supposed to be going to San Diego." Grey called from the back room.

"San Diego?" I muttered in confusion. I stormed into the office to consult my emails and my planner.

Sure enough I had reserved a space at the San Diego winter bridal convention back in September. I hadn't bought a plane ticket or reserved a room though. Time and heartache had distracted me.

So I plopped back down in front of my laptop to do just that.

"What's wrong?" Grey asked surprising me while I went through my convention stuff.

I was in the garage, sitting on the concrete floor next to my car. My back was facing the interior garage door and the washer and dryer (they were going at the moment). I was also crying again.

I just shook my head afraid to speak.

Grey crept around the car to avoid the bins of pamphlets, business cards and other items I used at conventions. He obviously wasn't taking my silence.

He squatted down in front of me.

I sighed sucking back my tears. I quickly wished that the pain would subside so Grey wouldn't see me like this.

"Can you count out a hundred pamphlets for me?" I asked him cheerfully; which even surprised me.

Grey didn't move.

"You do know I can see through your magic? What's happened to upset you, little Jinn?" he remarked moving the Tupperware bin aside to sit down in front of me.

I was always someone's 'little Jinn'. Andrea called me little Jinn. Grey called me little Jinn. Most importantly Rune called me his little Jinn.

Crying again.

"Did Andrea come back?" Grey asked and then answered his own question. "No. But it *is* a guy. You don't have to go into it."

Grey got to his feet and started to go back the way he came.

"Grey..." I whispered with so many questions about little Jinns like me.

He turned around to wait on me.

"What happened to all of the female love Jinn? There had to be a lot back when Jinx became one." I asked wiping away the tears and forcing out a smile.

Grey looked a little confused by my question.

"It would be nice to chat with another female Jinn about her experiences. I mean I don't have a lot of female friends you know." I added using my charm on him and hoping it worked.

"Female love Jinns were ruled solely by their hearts. They had protectors but their protectors tended to fall in love with them. There were all sorts of issues associated with female love Jinn. There had never been a lot of them to begin with..." Grey said in a sort of resignation.

"So like Lilith and Eve we were nothing but trouble?" I asked feeling useless suddenly. I decided to move on to counting pamphlets to concentrate on something else.

"But worth it. Worth every issue, every trying task. And do you know why?" Grey said with a confident smile.

I gazed up at him hopefully waiting on the answer.

"Because the female love Jinn that can be properly guided is a prize to behold. She will be strong and worthy of high praise in the High Goddess' court. A female love Jinn can repopulate the world with other female love Jinn. But there are males that are against it because some have fallen prey to females." Grey explained coming to squat down in front of me.

Was that why Rune had stopped calling? Maybe Conrad warned him against me at the last moment? Maybe he didn't want to be tainted by me?

"There's more useless stuff right now in all of those letters your ancestors wrote. Just know I'm here as your protector. You will persevere." Grey said patting me on the head before he went to check on his partner Damascus.

I checked into the lovely Marriott Marquis & Marine on Harbor in San Diego the next morning after leaving Jacksonville in the early afternoon. The hotel was beautiful and right down the street from the San Diego convention center. I patted myself on the back physically for a job well done on short notice as I peeked out of my window after the street at the Pacific Ocean.

My iPhone suddenly began ringing on the table beside me. I was tempted to let it keep ringing. Since I left Jacksonville a strange number kept calling me and hanging up before the voice mail could take a message.

Finally I answered the call.

"Thank you for calling Eden. This is Jinx Heydan, how may I help you?"

"Finally, baby! What are you doing? Screening your calls?" Rune blurted out.

My heart seized in my chest recognizing his voice.

"Me? I'm sorry...I'm the one that has been calling and leaving messages for a week...asshole." I retorted bitterly, moving away from the window as I felt the tears begin to choke me.

"Asshole?" Rune repeated and then he must have realized that I was pissed because he got silent for a minute.

"I deserve that. Will you let me explain before you give me the goodbye speech?" he said sounding a little choked up too.

"Fine. Explain." I demanded in Greek. The words just came out like that.

"My love, right after you left I lost my phone. Well not lost. I stopped at Starbuck's with you that morning and when I got home to call you I realized that my phone was gone. I went back to Starbuck's to see if someone turned it in. No one did and I tried to wait it out but days went by arguing with AT&T and all. I just ended up getting a new phone and number. My old number should be re-activated on this phone tomorrow. You're the first person I called. I was dead in the water without my phone." Rune explained back in Greek between a sniffle here and a sniffle there.

"You had my business card with my email address and all..." I insisted feeling a tear trickle down my right cheek.

"My angel, I threw away the card when I programmed your information into my phone. I kept trying to call you but I had the numbers mixed up. I am so sorry. I should have known something stupid would come between us." Rune said sincerely. I could feel the pain in his voice.

"I hope you put my information somewhere else for a backup in case it happens again." I sighed, finding some tissue to blow my nose. "I missed you so much, Rune."

I could hear Rune break down on his end.

"I miss you so much, Jinx. Tell me what I've missed. What are you wearing? What are you doing? Maybe we should Facetime." Rune sighed anxiously.

"Facetime definitely." I agreed so ready to see his beautiful face.

So we hung up and tried to Facetime each other at the exact same time a few times. After four times I sent him a text and told him to try again and I'd wait.

That time we finally got to see each other. His blue eyes were watery from obvious tears and I definitely wished I was there to hold him (or he was here with me).

"Holy shit! What did you do?" Rune exclaimed suddenly standing in front of me with his phone in his hand.

I was so happy to see him I wrapped my arms around him tightly.

After he got over the shock of being zapped from one coast to the next he wrapped his arms around me. His mouth found mine and it was over from there.

SIXTEEN

We woke up around dinnertime after two hours of lovemaking and passing out. It was dark out but the bay front was bustling. We could see that from the window. We were both naked peeking out from behind the curtain on the fifth floor.

"Where are we?" Rune asked kissing my bare right shoulder as we looked out at the pedestrians.

"San Diego. I have a bridal convention tomorrow." I answered putting my head back on his chest.

Rune made a thoughtful sound, holding me close.

"I haven't been here since the mid-seventies. We should go out and hit the town," he added turning me around in his arms to face him.

"Can you spend the night?" I asked timidly, resting my forehead against Rune's chest.

"I can but I have to go in the morning. I have a sitting." Rune answered kissing the top of my head.

"Would I have to wish you home?" I asked gazing up at him. Because if it was up to me he wouldn't be going anywhere.

"I can wish myself home, my little devil. But now you've discovered a new trick, right?" he smiled down at me.

"That means that I can go to you or you to me in an instant. Right? That's cool, right? Why didn't you do that when you lost your phone?" I inquired with uncertainty.

"It's very cool and I'm glad you've learned this. I didn't do it because I didn't want to scare the shit out of you like you just did to me. But let's put that lesson behind us and let's see San Diego in 2015." Rune smiled from his eyes to his mouth.

I smiled back, grabbing some clothes and running to the shower. Rune got in with me, really distracting me from washing. I just wanted to wash him and touch him; which he patiently allowed. But then when Rune tried to make love to me and my "shop" had closed we got out to get dressed.

Rune wished himself a pair of dark denim jeans, black boots and a black and white horizontal striped sweater to wear.

I shrugged on some light blue jeans, black ankle boots and a white tank top under a loose off-the-shoulder purple sweater. It wasn't cold when I came in so I figured I wouldn't be freezing now. At least that's what I was hoping.

I grabbed my purse and room key, ready to go. Rune grabbed my hand and we headed out.

Rune seemed to have a really good memory of San Diego as we strolled from bar to club.

And we had a great time, always within a hands-stretch from each other. I barely wanted to leave his side to use the ladies' room because I was so afraid he was going to disappear. Because during those days that he was incommunicado I had dreams that he was there and then gone.

Anyway I had to use the ladies room in the third club. When I came back out this blonde female was whispering something into Rune's ear. He smiled, grabbed the female's arm and pulled her close. I just froze (not in a good way) and that crazy jealous feeling (I had at night thinking Rune was fucking someone else) crept down my spine.

Just keeping walking Jinx. Walk right past him and out of his life, my conscience told me.

So I did. I was about five steps out of the bathroom before a hand reached out from the shadows to grab me. Then I was pulled back into the shadows for a kiss.

"You were taking forever. I thought you fell in." Rune whispered into my right ear as he kissed down my neck.

I stared back at where I thought Rune should have been and a man with Rune's thick hair and the blonde were kissing.

"How did you do that?" I uttered curtly, tensing up against his embrace.

"What are you talking about? Who are you glaring at?" Rune asked, physically turning my face to look at him.

"That's you with the blonde at the stool you were sitting. I know your smile." I stated unable to look him in the eyes because of my jealousy.

Rune looked back in the direction I was glaring. I looked back too and saw something

117

completely different. An older couple possibly mid-fifties were standing there making out. Huh? And ew!

Rune looked back at me dumbfounded.

"I don't look anywhere like that man." Rune remarked hesitantly. The look in his eyes told me something unseen was at work here.

Rune took me by the hands and lead the way out of the club.

"Has that ever happened to you before?" he asked me once we were outside.

"Has what ever happened to me before?" I asked really confused by the question and how quickly the scene changed inside.

"That was magic in there." Rune stated pointing back at the club.

I eyed him skeptically. "Magic? Yeah...yours."

"No. Not mine. That magic was specifically focused on you. I have no reason to deceive you and that magic was deceitful." Rune remarked seriously, pulling me farther away from the club.

"What are you saying? You didn't have some blonde whispering in your ear that you grabbed her possessively into making out? He had your...smile." I snapped and then faltered thinking of the heart-wrenching moment again. It had to have been Rune with that female and somehow he was able to be in two places at once.

"I followed you to the ladies room, hoping no one else would go in and then I could sneak in to make love to you. But some other women went in after you so I just waited for you to come out. When you did you looked for me and then I came

118

up behind you. Some other couple probably took my seat when I got up. I was never entertaining any blonde." Rune informed me as we walked.

I didn't believe him. Deep down I did but on the scathing surface after sleepless nights I didn't. Even though I knew he said he couldn't lie to me I had my doubts. Doubts that I didn't feel like expressing to anyone like Grey.

"I'm sorry if you feel like I'm accusing you. Maybe I drank too much." I said stiffly, giving up on any charm and charisma.

Rune pulled me into a wall where he kissed me hotly. His hands went up my arms and into my sweater and under my bra. I was almost certain that pedestrians could see what he was doing. I squeezed my eyes shut, attempting to focus on him, to ignore the feelings of betrayal and doubt. It was hard to do until I felt my sweater go up over my head and my bra disappear.

"Rune?" I gasped opening my eyes in alarm.

"Mmmm…" Rune mumbled with my nipple in his mouth.

We weren't on the street anymore. We were back in the Marriott hotel room against the door.

I conceded, feeling safe and out of public view. I conceded my anger too, giving it up for the passion I felt for Rune. Passion and how crazy I was about him.

I woke up hours later with a wake-up call and my phone alarm. I reached beside me for Rune's warmth to find him gone. I rolled over to face his pillow just to make sure I hadn't imagined the whole thing.

I hadn't. The pillow smelled like Rune's Suave shampoo. I sighed as the January morning sunshine beamed through the open curtains onto my face.

Then I sat up to find a little note now on my lap.

Rune.

"I hated to leave you but work is work. Last night was magnificent. I missed you so much. I miss you still. I hope that you'll come see me when the convention is over, my angel. My number should be on your phone. Try either of them just in case. My heart is with you.

Rune"

It was written in Greek which was cool. I hadn't brought any of my foreign language puzzle books with me on this trip to practice my languages so this worked.

I put the note in my purse and got ready for the day.

SEVENTEEN

Three hours later I took a break from my booth to stroll around and meet new possible comrades. One of the things I loved most about going to conventions was making new contacts. Even if I didn't make one new client a convention was worth it to hob-knob with other fellow wedding planners and who-have-you.

I looked for people I already knew from other conventions like DeeDee from Sandals; but DeeDee wasn't there (thankfully. We don't exactly get along). Instead one of her fellow employees Bekkah was. So I stopped to chat with her about Sandals' new resort in Jamaica.

"Do you have any other resorts that aren't in Jamaica?" I asked the same question most of my clients ask.

Bekkah jumped up gleefully to snatch up a new brochure.

"Grenada! Sandals LaSource Grenada! It's different!" Bekkah piped.

"Grenada? I haven't been there yet." I smiled taking the brochure to peruse it a bit.

"Oh my God! You have to come see it. Would you like for me to put you on a guest list?"

Bekkah gushed excitedly, going to a clipboard on her table.

For a small time wedding planner and travel agent I did refer a good lot of business to Sandals and Beaches alike. It wasn't my favorite vacation resort; however I got a lot of free stays there. But Grenada might be nice. I'd never been there seriously.

"Sure. Can I have a few more brochures?" I responded cheerfully, suddenly imagining a romantic weekend in Grenada with Rune.

Bekkah handed me ten more brochures and I took one of Bekkah's business cards before moving on to another booth.

Amazingly enough there was a designer dressmaker. A dressmaker in a booth two away from Bekkah. I was still interviewing to find the best dressmaker for Pippa Lancaster's vintage wedding gown. And this dressmaker...her specialty was vintage.

"I'm just starting out. My sister recommended that I try out one of these conventions," the black girl told me as I reviewed her sketches.

"Have you made these?" I asked curiously but still very interested in this girl's work.

"I made one to look like the gown Audrey Hepburn wore to the ambassador's ball in My Fair Lady. My cousin had a friend that was totally into Audrey Hepburn," the girl said anxiously.

"I need a dress that someone would have worn in the twenties." I said still flipping pages of her portfolio. In flipping I found exactly what I was looking for already completed. "This is exactly what I was imagining."

The girl asked if it was for me and I told her no.

"I'm a wedding planner. Jinx Heydan. My client in England is looking for a dress just like this one. Is this one available?" I added brightly, tapping on the picture.

The girl looked at the picture upside down.

"I could never find anyone to buy that one. It was my first. I call it Zelda F."

"How much do you want for it?" I asked taking my phone out to take a picture of the dress. Then I sent it to Pippa for her opinion.

"Five hundred fifty dollars..." the girl said between confidence and uncertainty.

"Will you be here for a while? I'm waiting for a response." I asked taking a mental note of the price.

The girl nodded. She was probably in her mid-twenties when I really looked at her. She reminded me of me when I started out.

"I'm Anita Kormin," she said extending her hand.

I shook it and told Anita that I'd be back before the end of the day.

I went back to my table just as two women came up. One woman with hair so black it was purple paused for a moment and then kept going. The other woman with golden hair stopped and I gave her my spiel while my phone hummed in the pocket of my black linen pants.

Her name was Amanda Morse and she was sweet. She was twenty-two and she had just got engaged. Her sister was not far behind her at another booth.

I gave Amanda my card just in case because she really had no clue what she wanted yet.

After Amanda and her sister ambled away I checked my voice mail.

It was Pippa. She was practically screaming into the message that she had to have that dress. Then I heard Landon in the background telling her that her dress limit was six hundred US dollars or three hundred fifty-seven British pounds. When you thought about it in pounds it always looks cheaper.

So I ended the message and tracked Anita down again, business credit card in hand. We did our transaction and I provided Anita with my P.O. Box to ship the dress. She called someone to have them package up the dress right away.

"Get a business card and send it to me. I'd be happy to mention you in my company blog. Publicity always helps." I added taking my receipt and went back to my table.

The woman with the purple hair had came back.

"Wedding planner?" the woman said with a crisp disdain.

"Or matchmaker. I also offer honeymoon services. It's not for everyone." I shrugged, brushing off her quip. I checked my phone and there was less than an hour left in the convention.

"Interesting. I'm a photographer," the woman said extending a hand.

"Covering the convention?" I asked simply, beginning to discretely pack up.

I remembered Rune's note. I wonder if that meant that I could wish myself and everything I brought with me to Atlanta, to Jacksonville. That would be so cool! I wouldn't have to pay for airlines anymore!

"Actually I'm a wedding photographer. I believe you know Rune Kalakos..." the woman answered breaking my wonderings with two words that stopped me in my tracks.

"Yes. I do. Do you?" I said not adding anything.

"Yes I do too. Beautiful with a bright smile. Crooked top front tooth," she said with this smile. It wasn't quite at the surface but waiting to burst forth.

All I could do was stare at this woman.

"Come have a drink with me. It won't take long. I only want to hear about him," the woman said offering her hand again.

"Why?" I uttered hesitantly.

"Rune and I are old friends. Tell me does he still pine after Semadar?" she finally smiled. I caught pointed lower canines briefly.

I stepped back.

"Oh! You don't know about Semadar. Oh! Come on! Have a drink with me. Say in the lobby of your hotel?" she grinned now.

The lower canines really unnerved me. What was she? Was she real?

Then again she also looked familiar like I'd seen her before.

Out of curiosity (and that nagging doubt that Rune wasn't true to me) I accepted her offer.

After I had packed everything up at the end of the convention I bid a hollow farewell to Anita and Bekkah. I wished it all home to Jacksonville before I stepped out of the convention center so I had less to worry about (I really hoped it all arrived safely including my clothes). Then I went back to the Marriott that I had checked out of this morning and found the bar.

The woman was sitting on the far end of the bar with a glass of something brown. It might have been whiskey or bourbon; but I didn't ask. I just took a seat one away from her and asked for a house Moscato (I wasn't sure if I would actually be able to drink it though).

"So is he still beautiful? I'm sure he is with that odd accent. Am I right?" the woman started, bringing the glass to her lips.

The bartender set the glass of wine in front of me.

"Who are you?" I asked putting my hands around the glass.

"I'm Sigyn. As I said an old friend of Rune's," she smiled eyeing me over her glass.

"Well, Sigyn, why don't you contact Rune yourself and ask him?" I said uncomfortably, attempting to take a sip of the house Moscato. Honestly I couldn't remember what the wine tasted like.

Sigyn grinned obviously trying to make out what I was thinking.

I sat there trying to understand why this woman had approached me.

"What do you know about Mr. Kalakos?" Sigyn asked me, putting her glass upside down on the cocktail napkin in front of her.

I shrugged. I wasn't going to add fuel to the fire, as they say. Sigyn had something she wanted to say and I was going to hear her out if she wanted to contribute.

Sigyn smiled. She never really stopped smiling or grinning like she held some sort of power over me.

"Let me start with Semadar then. If I had to deal with her you should too." Sigyn said ignoring my obvious discomfort with the subject.

"Semadar...she wasn't even around when Rune and I met. I'm not going to say she was dead or not in existence because she's probably out there right now laughing at us." Sigyn laughed, tapping the bar with her two-inch long index fingernail. The bartender placed another tumbler in front of her.

"Why is she laughing at us?" I asked simply. Who was Semadar? Who the hell was Sigyn? And why did I really have to know?

"Did you know that Rune was a companion of Alexander the Great? He told me once that he knew *the* Alexander the Great. You know your history?" she remarked softly, slipping into the seat next to me.

"I know about my history. I'm Persian. I know who Alexander the Great is." I started stiffly.

I didn't want her to be near me. And how did Sigyn know Rune hung out with Alexander?

"Rune wasn't just his companion. One of Alexander's tours took him to the border of Asia and the known Persian empire. He collected treasures. One was this spectacular lamp. Alexander took the lamp back to his camp and soon after Rune came to Alexander as the guardian of the lamp. That peaked Alexander's curiosity and Rune being the responsible one explained the lamp's properties. Alexander woke the lamp and out came Semadar. She became Alexander's sex slave instead of love Jinn." Sigyn gushed.

I held up my hand to interrupt her.

"How do you know about love Jinns?"

"Just what Rune told me." Sigyn remarked with a casual hug.

"Why would he tell you about love Jinns?" I asked with a sinking suspicion.

"I told you. We were old friends..." Sigyn said again but I heard something different.

"Anyway Semadar was in love with two men and only one was in love with her – Rune. He told me that he was so in love that he asked to become a love Jinn as a way to protect Semadar better. It was granted and irreversible. But Semadar gave up her love Jinn status to help Alexander with war and glory. Rune said he was devastated and it was important that I understood her importance to him." Sigyn continued whether I wanted to hear it or not.

I abruptly paid for my wine and excused myself for the ladies' room. She had the upper hand and I wasn't going to sit there through that. I could be a patient and compassionate person but this chick had completely screwed me up.

I stepped into a stall, infuriated and humiliated. But I didn't fuss and cry in a lobby restroom. I wished myself directly to Rune (wherever his ass was).

EIGHTEEN

Rune!" I shouted angrily, standing in the middle of his studio office.

I shouted his name again, so pissed off that I didn't even consider the time or the situation. I just knew that I wished to be exactly where he was and I ended up here.

Rune flew into the office pleasantly surprised to find me. He probably thought I was here as an answer to his note. The jerk!

"Jinx!" he beamed stepping towards me.

"Don't come near me! Who in the hell is Sigyn?" I demanded putting a wall of glass up between him and me with a wish (of course).

"Sigyn?" he repeated in confusion.

"Yeah. The chick that's "an old friend" but she knows things you decided not to tell me?" I quipped darkly.

I've never truly been angry in my life. Never. I've been frustrated in thirty-one years; dismally disappointed in thirty-one years. But I've never been angry enough to spit fire (as Grandma Nasira used to say).

"An old friend? You're not making any sense, Jinx." Rune replied shaking his head but keeping his distance from the glass wall.

"Sure I am. Why would you tell 'an old friend' that you were a love Jinn? Why would you tell her about being in love with another love Jinn?" I continued just growing in fury (I felt like Jean Grey as the Phoenix. That's why I thought of the word fury).

"I'm really confused. Do you mind going back to the beginning? If I'm going to be interrogated." Rune replied, beginning to rub his temples. He took a seat on the couch I had sat on once or twice.

"What does that matter? Why is she telling me about Semadar? The stuff she said is talked about with either a best friend or a lover. She's not your best friend. She's not old enough to be your best friend. And she kept talking about how beautiful you are." I seethed. I was pretty close to spitting that fire.

Rune stopped, rubbing his temples when I said *her* name. He had lied!

The glass wall shattered into dust and I broke down in tears, falling into the chair in front of Rune's desk.

Rune shot to his feet, coming to grab me up into his arms.

"Jinx…" he whispered, holding me so close that we could have been one.

"I don't know who this devil is that's trying to come between us but I'm not going to allow it," he added teetering us back to the couch.

Rune sat down with me curled into his lap.

"But she knew you. She told me about Alexander…" I insisted not giving up on the fact that Rune had lied.

131

I cannot lied to you as a love Jinn. But he didn't start out as a love Jinn...

Rune exhaled heavily and heaved a sob.

"How dare you cry? All you've done is lie to me!" I spat out so ready to slap him as I pulled away from him.

"I never lied to you. Give me a chance," he stated wiping away a few tears.

"I have and you lied." I snapped getting to my feet awkwardly.

I was a millisecond from wishing myself home and then in a blink of my eye I couldn't move (Rune!) and I couldn't speak.

"I have power too, Jinx. I cannot lie to you. We've known each other a few weeks. Over time I would tell you more about me like you will tell me about you." Rune said solemnly, slowing coming into view in front of me.

"I don't know any Sigyns. I have never shared my secrets with anyone. You are the only person I've told about being a love Jinn," he said standing there beginning to tear up again.

God! He was so beautiful and sad standing there. He looked conflicted and I think he should have. He hadn't told me everything; but then again why would he?

"I told you because I know we'll be together a very long time. We had all the time in the world to reveal our stories. And we still do...if you will just hear me out. If you would just trust me because you're in love with me." Rune stated holding in a sob.

I could finally move and I started to cry again.

"I am." I whispered reaching up to touch Rune's face.

Rune grabbed my hand, holding it there.

"I'm in love with you. I should know better like I said; but I am. And yes, her name was Semadar. Her new name became something Alexander chose. I fell in love with her and I was her protector...only her protector," he continued as his tears fell onto my hand.

Grey had mentioned that protectors ended up falling for their charges when I asked about female love Jinn.

"Are you a protector or a love Jinn, Rune?" I asked still feeling a lot of pain. I saw the sword in Rune's hands New Year's morning when I surprised him.

Rune took my hand from his face. Then he led me back to the couch. He pulled me down next to him to face him.

He took a couple deep breathes to steady and calm his nerves.

"As I said I was born in Macedonia when Alexander of Macedonia was sixteen. My mother said I would be special. She never told me that she belonged to several men in the tribe; but she knew my father wasn't of this earth. I thought she was crazy until my father came to claim me. He was a Jinn protector of one lamp. He trained me and told me that I should continue to protect this lamp and its Jinn inside. He told me more but it's the same thing Grey could tell you."

I listened and breathed. Really I was trying to commune with the Jinx I knew I was. The lover not the fighter.

"So I protected the lamp from the moment my father gave the lamp to me. He ran off to commit the rest of his life to my mother (it was a trade). I didn't know who was in the lamp but I was an awful protector or maybe I was just scared off by a thousand troops ransacking the village the lamp resided. Alexander's chiefs found the lamp and took it back to him. I followed the lamp, waited for a private moment to introduce myself to Alexander and from then on was his companion."

"When did you trade off protector for love Jinn?" I asked seeing some thoughts run across Rune's mind that kept him from speaking.

"Alexander finally called on the lamp and out came Semadar, the love Jinn. She tried to explain her purpose; but Alexander saw her as a pretty thing and he didn't want love magic. He wanted glory and power so he used her as a sex slave. I tried to protect her as best as I could, guiding her. But she was appeared sweet and very pretty (not as stunning as you). She was a Hebrew turned slave she told me. Anyway she enchanted me and so I did what I could to be with her; including sharing her with Alexander. And slowly she started using her magic to get me to do her work so she could get me out of the way. She also used her magic to bewitch Alexander and his chiefs. She became drunk on this power she had over the men. I went to the Council to request that I became a love Jinn to show Semadar reason; to show how a love Jinn should be." Rune continued, reaching out to touch my face with both hands.

"I didn't do it so she would love me. It was the only way I could see reigning Semadar in after talking to other protectors like Conrad. But the Council granted my wish and taught me what I needed to do. Conrad became my protector and I went back to Semadar on the eve of an important battled for Alexander. I tried to stop her..." Rune explained as tears came down his cheeks again.

"Did you feel about her like you do about me?" I asked because I didn't want to draw out his pain. I just wanted to know how much I had to contend with when it came to Semadar. I wasn't sure how to deal with Sigyn yet.

First things first.

"No. Semadar was a first conquest. We were both young and naïve. It was never a connection thing. We never chatted together like we do." Rune responded with a shaky sigh.

"So why does she bother you?" I asked and then I answered my own question. "Because you failed her."

"I failed her terribly even if centuries and Conrad have told me otherwise. Besides it was horrible to see her change from sweet love Jinn to something else. After she changed she was zapped from our existence, probably to learn her new life. The next day Alexander won the battle and I brought him his first wife when he asked to see the eligible women. I then occupied Semadar's lamp when Alexander had no need of me." Rune concluded with a tremor.

I pulled him into my arms and held him, hoping to forget why I was pissed with him.

"I needed you here today…" Rune whispered ten minutes later pulling away from me after a sweet kiss.

"What's happened?" I asked softly, deciding to focus solely on Rune. If I thought about beautiful Rune I hoped to ignore anything else.

"The couple in the negative I showed you…" he began looking me in the eyes.

I nodded, recalling the couple and the negative.

"The girl is in critical condition with some mystery disease. The guy has been committed to a mental relaxation center." Rune informed me flatly.

I stared at him, dumbfounded. "What?"

"I called like you suggested to offer a free sitting and free portraits. It took several attempts; but Jill got through to someone watching their place. They told her what had happened and she told me before she left for the day." Rune said sitting back against the back of the couch. He started rubbing his temples again. That must be what Rune did when he was frustrated; I jut got some wine.

"Can we go back to your place to discuss this more?" I asked suddenly, wanting some wine that I hoped Rune would have.

Rune snapped his fingers and we were sitting on the brown leather sectional in his living room. Two glasses of Moscato were sitting on the redwood claw-footed coffee table in front of us.

NINETEEN

Is this what you were thinking?" Rune asked taking a glass to hand to me.

"How did you do that? Snap and all." I said in awe, taking a sip of some really good Moscato.

"I told you I'm just like you only I like to give some warning before I transport some place. Now back to the problem at hand..." Rune smiled faintly, probably feeling more at home in his own living room.

I wished that his studio looked closed for the day just in case he didn't.

"Do you use your magic often? For transportation?" I just had to know.

"Sometimes..." Rune uttered with a little grin, raising his glass in a toast before he took a sip.

"OK. Keep your secrets." I pouted shoving him gently.

"Jinx, I think it's my fault that something has happened to my clients." Rune said growing all serious again.

"How?" I asked emphatically.

"I don't know. I think that's why the negatives look like they do." Rune shrugged putting his glass down to put his head in his hands.

"That doesn't make sense, baby. You just took their picture. How can you be responsible? What? You zapped them with radiation or something? You can't be responsible. What I want to sort out is that chick Sigyn. Why is she taking aim at me? Or even you." I replied speaking sensibly now.

All the anger and resentment had left me. I trusted Rune. Well at least I did when he was with me and he could talk me off the ledge.

"That's what she said her name was? Sigyn?" Rune asked getting up like I had struck a nerve.

"Yeah. Sigyn. She said she was a photographer when she first introduced herself. She didn't tell me her name until I met her for drinks (because I thought it made sense). Anyway she had purplish black hair and scary teeth." I told him putting my glass down too.

Rune gestured that I follow him upstairs to his guest room/home office.

"Sigyn was the name of Loki's faithful wife. The Norse named her a goddess; but no one knows of what. To what purpose did she serve." Rune commented as he rummaged through papers on his desk. His home office was the exact opposite of his real office (basically it was a mess in here).

"Loki? How do you know that?" I asked wishing I had brought my wine with me. The glass appeared in my right hand. Man! I loved being a Jinn.

"Another story for another day. Remember…we have forever." Rune remarked still sorting through papers.

I shrugged. OK. I got that.

"So what are you looking for?"

"When you said the name again it sounded familiar."

"In your bills?" I uttered.

Rune nodded with his back to me. My eyes found their way to his butt. His jeans looked really really good on him.

Back to the problem at hand, Jinx, my conscience told me.

"Anything in your bills talk about scary teeth?" I asked sipping my wine carefully. I could feel myself getting drunker by the moment. I didn't eat today I just realized.

"Scary teeth?" Rune repeated in confusion, digging and sorting.

"Yeah scary teeth. She had lower canines like the Sabretooth from the second X-Men. Do you know what I mean?" I attempted to find a valid correlation and I came up with Sabretooth from X2. What a dork I am!

"I preferred Live Schreiber's version. Every time I see him I think he still looks like Sabre-tooth." Rune remarked understanding my reference. Yay!

"Found it!" Rune declared a second later, holding up an invoice.

I stepped over to hand him my glass of wine and plucked the slip from his hands. I perused the slip to see that this was the purchase receipt for the brand new lens he bought the day before we met.

"See the name at the bottom?" Rune said drawing my attention lower on the invoice.

My eyes sort of crossed and my vision got blurry. But I made out the name Sigyn.

"You bought the lens from her? Ok..." I said attempting to look up at Rune; but I still felt my eyes cross.

"Did you eat today? Are you drunk?" Rune asked curiously, putting the glass and the invoice on the desk.

"No and I don't think so." I answered shaking my head. The room kind of tilted and Rune caught me.

The next thing I knew I was sitting up in Rune's heavy Louis V style queen bed. I was in a white lace slip (that I didn't own) being hand fed crackers and fruit.

"You needed something in your stomach. Good thing your man is here to take care of you." Rune smiled when I finally focused on his face.

"Did I pass out?" I asked after he handed me a bottle of water from the bedside table.

"For an hour or so. I just woke you up." Rune shrugged, holding another bite of apple in his hands.

"Did you figure out anything about Sabretooth Sigyn?" I asked sipping the water.

"Only that she sold me the camera lens I've been using for the past two weeks. I looked her up while you were asleep..." Rune said handing me the rest of the apple slice.

"And…" I pressed anxiously. I had to know why this woman was trying to mess with my relationship.

"The website that's on the invoice doesn't exist anymore. I tried to look it up – nothing. I Googled her and nothing came up. I'm thinking dead end," he informed me.

I frowned and kept eating the crackers on the plate in Rune's lap.

Because we had nothing else to go on we laid in Rune's bed holding hands while speculating on who Sigyn was. But then the conversation went to our favorite X-Men which had nothing to do with strange dark-haired women with scary teeth. Then we passed out tucked into each other's arms.

The next afternoon I went home when five alerts went off on my phone (that was in my pocket) related to work. Rune promised to call when he was done with the wedding he had.

One of my alerts was a major one – finding a reception site for Billy and Tamara. Tamara must have had a reminder set up for herself because she called me before I had even turned on my laptop.

Damascus met me in the office and Grey wasn't home (but he did have a real job – police detective).

"Are we having the service in a church?" Tamara asked me while I unlocked my laptop and got out their file.

I flopped it open and both spots for service and reception were blank. Ugh!

"Let's recap what we've done so far. OK?"
I said so we could both get reacquainted with the
process. It had been maybe three weeks since we
had seen each other last.

I went over the facts that we had the
dresses, shoes, veil and colors. We had a date
March seventeenth. We had the florist because
we did that when I was in Rock Hill for the final
dress fitting.

"Oh! I remember now. Billy wasn't sure
about a church. We don't attend one so that
would be awkward, right? What do you suggest?"
Tamara recalled suddenly.

I vaguely recalled Billy mentioning that
during our first meeting at their condo clubhouse.

"We could always get two conference
rooms at a hotel: one for the service and one for
the reception. Or maybe a place that has indoor
and outdoor space." I suggested opening my
Chrome browser to look up Rock Hill.

"Indoor/outdoor? What's that mean?"
Tamara inquired curiously.

"I just did a wedding on New Year's Eve at
a resort in Portugal. The service was done on the
beach and the reception was held in the banquet
room. Indoor…outdoor…" I replied cheerfully,
clicking on hotels in Rock Hill.

Tamara squealed with excitement. "Oh
my God! Let me call Billy and tell him what you
suggested! I'll call you right back!"

Click!

Damascus lifted his head off of his paws
and shook it. The call was on speaker so the
squeal probably hurt his ears.

142

"I know." I said reaching over to pat his head.

I continued to research possible multi purpose sites.

For the next four hours I worked on four weddings and my matchmaking. I felt like I was really slacking on my dating site so I blocked tomorrow out to work solely on the matchmaking. I probably wasn't slacking but I felt that way.

But after work Damascus and I took a walk. Then we got in the car to pick up sushi that I ordered while we walked. When we came back we ate and settled in for the night (Grey didn't show up that I knew).

Rune called before I went to bed. He told me that he stopped using his new lens and went back to his old one. He said he was testing a theory. I still didn't think his clients' illnesses were his fault. How could they be?

But I fell asleep after hearing Rune's voice. I slept just as good as last night and woke up ready for the day.

<u>TWENTY</u>

I had a couple great nights of sleep; some of them Rune actually spent with me (either I went to him or he came to me). Since I was sleeping good I got a lot of work done. I even found a multi purpose site for Billy and Tamara, reserved it and started working on the cake.

Travelling got a whole lot easier too since I had learned to discretely pop from place to place. I waited on Grey to fuss at me about my use of magic but I didn't see him so much. I mean I could take Damascus with me to Rune's so there was no need to leave him all of the time.

Yep! Everything was going great for about two weeks.

After two weeks I had gone down to Orlando to personally pick up Pippa's gown that Anita had shipped a while ago. I had been lazy and I had to turn around and ship the gown to Pippa.

"So that's what I needed. I'm having it overnighted to you. When you get it call me. I have a seamstress that can alter it if need be." I was telling Pippa while I completed the shipping label at the FEDEX store.

My phone chose that moment to beep with an incoming call. I pulled the phone away from my right ear to see Violet was calling. Well I couldn't answer right then. If it was important she'd call back.

"And you'll be out here to do the cake and florist thing in two weeks? Landon decided late May was better." Pippa asked nervously.

"Yes. I have you two on my calendar. Just call me the second the dress arrives, OK, Pippa?" I stated brightly but hurriedly, pressing the label against the box evenly so it wouldn't come off.

Pippa said absolutely and we hung up.

I gave the box to the FEDEX rep confidently, asking for insurance and signed delivery. I was terrified that something would happen to this one-of-a-kind gown. I never felt like that before; but it was probably because I had been slacking. The dress could have been to Pippa a week ago if I wasn't so focused on Rune and matchmaking.

My phone rang again.

"Hey Vi! What's up?" I chirped answering this call.

"Jinxie! I'm home!" Violet exclaimed excitedly.

I handed Trey (the rep) my business credit card in disbelief.

"From work? That's great. What's happened that you're so excited?" I responded smiling politely at Trey while I waited on my receipt. Internally I groaned because Violet calling reminded me that I had receipts to sort out and scan to her. I tried to keep my finances in order monthly. Ugh! Not to mention tax time was coming fast.

"No silly. I'm home. I'm even hugging Damascus. He's gotten big. Do you know why it smells like a guy's cologne in my room? Did Andrea move in?" Violet gushed between giggles.

I dropped my phone on the counter dumbfounded.

Trey handed my receipt to me with my card. He grabbed the box and moved on to help the next customer.

I took what Trey gave me and picked up my phone.

"Say what? How?" I stammered going out to get in my Altima.

"I know! Isn't it great? Oh my God! I have to call Mom and Dad! Let me call them and I'll see you when you get here!" Violet piped ending the call.

I drove from Orlando to home as quickly as humanly possible. I could have popped me and the car home (I'm sure) but I needed the time to make sense of Violet's appearance.

When I got home I heard a voice I hadn't head in a while. Kyle Bach's.

I closed the electric garage door and stepped into my little foyer. Damascus came bounding up to me and running back to Violet's room.

"Jinx?" Violet called inching around the corner tentatively.

"It's me." I said so surprised to actually find her there.

A heartbeat passed. Then we ran to each other for a big hug.

"Oh! I missed you so much!" we both said at the same time.

Kyle appeared from the hall, shaking his head and smiling. He had a mustache and a beard now.

"Jinxie! It was so romantic!" Violet exclaimed, leading me into the kitchen.

Oh! The good old days when we would talk about our day over a glass of wine. I got a little teary eyed as I stood there watching her.

Kyle came in after me to retrieve three wineglasses. Violet pulled a bottle of champagne out of the fridge triumphantly.

I tried to stay out of the way as they filled glasses with champagne.

"We're still talking about the creepy cryptic countdown?" I remarked finding my voice again.

"Only you." Kyle chuckled, handing me a glass nonetheless.

"It *was* a little weird, baby." Violet added having my back. She'd have my back every now and again against Kyle.

"I thought you'd like the game. It was nerve-wrecking for me because I wasn't sure everything was going to work out." Kyle said with a shrug, getting the third glass for himself.

"So why are we having champagne?" I asked leaning against the counter with the microwave.

Violet held up her left hand so I could see the engagement ring from Skype in person.

I had my glass to my lips and I couldn't drink. She was engaged to Kyle?!

"I proposed properly. Don't worry, Jinx." Kyle added in my silence.

"Forget properly. Did you mean it?" I responded putting the glass down. "Did you mean to say yes, Violet?"

Kyle and Violet had dated for two years. Almost every day Violet made it known that she wanted to get married to stay in the country. Kyle made it known he didn't want to marry anyone and he had problems with Muslims and people from the Middle East.

If you also recall I was going to bomb Kyle if he married Violet.

Kyle put his arm around my shoulders and guided me around Violet to the kitchen table. Damascus trotted in to witness what happened next.

"I know I've seemed like an ass to you, Jinx. I want to apologize to you (I've already apologized to Vi). I was such an idiot but I see the truth now. I didn't understand or want to understand Muslims and the real people of the Middle East. I understand now. Just a couple months over there was all it took," he informed me gesturing to my glass of champagne.

I eyed him suspiciously over my glass.

"Then when Kyle got my message that I was moving to Cairo he made up his mind. On my birthday he came to my uncle's office and proposed." Violet added brightly, drinking her champagne.

"She didn't even recognize me." Kyle laughed retrieving his glass.

"Well I've never seen you with facial hair. Give me a break." Violet scoffed pushing at her fiancé.

They laughed and told me more about what transpired.

Two hours later I turned in for the night with Damascus. I didn't expect a call from Rune because I had talked to him this morning. He was going to check on a few of his clients that he had photographed with the new camera. After that he was meeting an old professor at Georgia Tech about the photo negatives.

So as I fell asleep I was anxious. Violet was back, engaged and I had no doubt that very soon she was going to ask me to plan her wedding. Kyle and Violet talked so much this evening that I also didn't have a chance to tell her what had been going on with me.

Oh well!

"Yes. Oh well, dear Jinx Hedayat," a familiar wry voice retorted in my dream, coming slowly into view.

There she was Miss Sabretooth. Exactly like I remembered her except we weren't sitting at a hotel bar.

I wasn't quite sure where we were and it was *my* dream. Or maybe it wasn't (especially if she was in it).

"What do you want? What are you?" I asked curtly, hoping to exude confidence.

"I want you to know the truth about your sweet and sexy Rune Kalakos." Sigyn smiled batting her long dark eyelashes.

It was then that I noticed her pupils were huge. Her eyes were nothing but pupil with a little bit of blue around the edges.

I don't think Sabretooth's eyes did that.

"I'll know the truth eventually. That's the beauty of being in a relationship. I should know..." I remarked with a smirk.

I bet she wasn't expecting that comeback. A bully can only intimidate you if you allow them.

"Because you're a love Jinn? Ha!" Sigyn scoffed starting to pace around me.

I looked straight ahead with my chin up, ignoring her. I realized that we were in the playground of the primary school I attended in Cairo. I loved that school.

"Actually I was thinking because I was a matchmaker." I said thinking fondly on the friends I had at this school. I smiled.

"Well little matchmaker love Jinn, would you like to know now or later that Rune is the one that's been against your family since the beginning?" Sigyn asked in my peripheral vision.

The smile left my face. Wait! What? Why would that upset me?

Oh! That's right! Grey said that someone kept the first Jinx from becoming a Jinn what-soever. But he did anyway so...?

"Doesn't that bother you? And then every step of the way going forward?" Sigyn continued in front of me now.

"It doesn't bother me. The inevitable still happened." I said with a shrug, smiling again.

Sigyn frowned and the playground scene faltered a bit. I really wanted to slide down the slide for old times sake.

"He was against you personally. He went to the Council to contest that *you* become a love Jinn. He tried to have your powers removed and if not he wanted to make sure you failed. He also said that your protector was insufficient. He was against you. I thought you should know that before you go off marrying him." Sigyn tried next.

Too late I changed the dream. I changed the dream but I couldn't shake the notion she was right.

TWENTY-ONE

I'm serious. I couldn't shake the notion that Sigyn was telling the truth. I know I seemed confident in my dream. I know! But that creepy chick got to me!

So when I woke up I needed to talk it out. Normally I talked it out with Damascus (since Violet had been gone) but he didn't offer any opinions. But now Vi was back...

I stumbled out of my bedroom, listening for another body.

Damascus was asleep in his corner of the couch so someone had let him out.

"Oh! That's a great idea! Do you think it will work?" Violet exclaimed blissfully (that's the only word to come to mind) as she came into view from the empty room.

In our house there was a room on the other side of the breakfast bar that we barely used. It was probably set up to be a family room originally; however Violet and I only used it for parties. That's where Violet and Kyle were standing.

"Guess what?" Violet beamed, waving me over in my Felix the Cat sleep pants and red matching top (I got it on a trip to the Islands of Adventure). Felix was creative like me.

"You guys already causing trouble on a Thursday morning?" I quipped going to start my Keurig instead.

Then I came back out to hear what Vi had to say.

"Kyle thinks that we should make this our office." Violet clapped her hands gleefully.

"It makes sense, right?" Kyle added gesturing to all of the empty space.

I stood back in the open space between the Great Room and the mystery room I had to mentally imagine what the space would be like as an office. It was a lot of space but I didn't need all of that room.

"You said 'our'..." I said curiously. I forgot there was always a catch when it involved Violet.

"I thought you girls could do your thing for real." Kyle suggested folding his arms over his chest. He was also in his pajamas. We all were.

I eyed them suspiciously. I went back into my current office to put my chai tea pod into my Keurig and hit Start.

They came and sat down on the loveseat before I could leave. No avoiding them. So I sat down in front of my desk to hear them out; even though I was really hoping to vent to Violet.

"Kyle and I were talking about what I will do for a living. He's still with the Bureau here unless he gets transferred. So he mentioned how well you were doing as a small businesswoman. And that got me thinking..." Violet said holding hands with Kyle. Her eyes glanced over to the

Keurig and that's where she paused. Bringing me chai tea in the morning used to be her job and then we'd work on the upcoming weddings.

"Vi could be her own accountant and your assistant. It makes her more flexible if I do have to move. Essentially it made sense that you guys set up in the empty room. Then this room could be a guest room or something." Kyle continued optimistically.

"I'll think about it while you guys decide if it's right for you." I said sensibly, reaching for my glass of chai tea which I took to the shower with me.

When I came back out Damascus was in the empty room chewing on his blue plastic bone. I went into the office to work.

About an hour later Violet appeared without Kyle.

"Still working on ten weddings" she asked with a treinta cup of chai tea from Starbuck's.

I nodded because I was in the middle of ordering the invitations for Billy and Tamara's wedding. I had to be very particular about the wording and the rush delivery. I had to concentrate because my mind was a whirl with new office ideas and this Sigyn thing.

"Something up?" Violet asked sometimes so astute when she wants to be.

I finished up the order and hit Submit.

Then I locked my computer screen so I could dump everything on Violet. I think it was safe now to tell Vi about Rune. Besides in order to tell her about my dream she had to know about him.

"Oh my God! That's awesome!" Violet shrieked when I got out the initial part of the story.

"I mean I'm sorry to hear about Andrea; but Rune sounds better than Andrea," she added hastily.

"Yeah...well Rune has deftly omitted certain important details. Like he had checked my background and knew all about me before we even met." I remarked rolling my eyes.

Violet's expression changed. The old Violet returned. The Violet that listened and understood and saw in shades of gray. The same Violet who took the news about doing weddings for vampires and Elfs like it was nothing (well other than believing all vampires were like the ones in True Blood).

"Uh...go back. How did he know about you? Is he 'special'?" Violet inquired all sorts of seriousness.

I wanted to just give her a squeeze.

So I just told her that he had the ability of foresight. I wasn't sure how much I could tell Vi about Jinn. Vi didn't know I was a Jinn so I wasn't going to tell her.

"Sometimes it's sweet when they look you up; but sometimes it screams 'stalker'. Do you think he did it for good reasons or bad?" Violet asked sitting back on the loveseat.

"I don't know. But just when I think I can trust him I can't." I groaned.

"Well trust is earned. Maybe you just need to hear him out. Men (and people) have many layers to them. You just got to peel them back." Violet said with a smile, placing her hands on her knees. Then she stood up.

"You should know that as a matchmaker. I mean would you make your clients spill all of their secrets at once? No. You give them grounds to get to know each other. They grow to trust each other, right?" Violet stated before she went to the office door.

"Think on that. I have to check on the whereabouts of my belongings. I'm not sure if I packed my planner or not." Violet added hopefully, going to her room.

I watched her go and did think about what she had said. Maybe she was right. Too bad my gut and heart were involved in an epic internal civil war.

Violet came back waving her planner in the air. So for now I was focused on working through these weddings with Violet. And at the end of the day Violet collected my receipts to start on that month's profit and loss.

I took Damascus out for a walk like we had been doing. Since I had such turmoil (I know big word) going on in my head Damascus and I walked out of the subdivision and down to the wooden bridge that crossed over JEA'S water intake creek. The walk gave me time to think.

"Boy! You must have a lot on your mind, walking all the way out here," a voice said breaking my concentration. Grey.

"Why can't we just be out here for exercise? We sit cooped up all day." I replied glancing down at Damascus who seemed to be enjoying this extended walk.

"Uh...you do realize that today was the coldest day of this winter...don't you?" Grey said hesitantly walking beside me.

"Your point is?" I asked not stopping to glance over at Grey. My mind was in desperate need of a wine overload and a mind swipe.

Grey grabbed Damascus' leash from my hand so I would have to stop and look at him.

So I did. Grey was wearing a heavy sweatshirt and sweatpants with sneakers. I, on the other hand, was wearing my BeBe cotton shorts and a thin gray sweater. I had flip-flops on my feet. Maybe he had a point.

Grey turned us all around to head back before I caught pneumonia (if that's even possible).

"What's got you so messed up? And don't lie to me again," he asked seriously.

"I've been seeing this guy – well he's another love Jinn. I thought he was genuinely interested in me; but I've been having doubts. And I met this scary chick who told me that this guy has known about me my whole life. All of our lives." I blurted out. I probably made no sense.

"Let's get back to your house and really talk. You're not making sense." Grey said confirming what I thought.

We walked in silence while I tried to think of how to tell Grey something that I didn't know how to say. I mean how would Grey take this? Would you tell me the truth? Would anyone tell me the truth because at this point I trusted no one.

157

My brain was about to implode. I could feel it. I was feeling emotions I wasn't used to feeling; at least I didn't think I ever had. I typically trusted until you proved me otherwise. I was definitely never jealous and 100% negative. These were the feelings overwhelming me.

When we got back to the house Violet was gone and she left a note that she was doing some shopping. She had a rental car to get her places until her Vespa was shipped from Egypt.

Grey poured me some wine and escorted me to my room. Damascus curled up on his pillow. Then Grey leaned against my footboard watching me sip the wine and waiting.

I sat on the edge of my bed still pondering what to say. The truth?

"I think I'm in love with another love Jinn that I met in Atlanta. His name (I think) is Rune Kalakos. He told me that he was a protector for Alexander's love Jinn (that's Alexander the Great) Semadar. He fell in love (or maybe he didn't) with her and to save her from those faults you mentioned females have he asked the Council to make him a love Jinn. The Council granted his wish and gave him his own protector Conrad. But when he came back to Semadar she granted a wish for glory for Alexander and she was changed into something else. Rune continued to be a love Jinn.

"But this crazy woman showed me that Rune keeps lying to me. For instance, she said Rune has been against me all along. She said he was trying to undermine me and you as my protector. I think she's telling the truth. Violet

158

thinks I just need to wait it out. She would say that now that she's engaged and happy with Kyle."

I stopped talking and really heard myself. Who was that talking to Grey? It couldn't have been me. I sounded so negative, so nasty and so miserable. I didn't like this person at all.

Grey must have noticed it too because he stepped back into my dresser. He eyed me suspiciously, then he reached out for my wine. He took it and refilled it and came back.

Two minutes later the front door opened and Vi was back.

"Kyle's bringing over sushi in a little bit! Just to let you know!" Vi called.

I clambered over my bed to say that was great, I'd be out soon. Then I closed my bedroom door and magically soundproofed the room.

"I assume you might or might not believe me if I told you (rather gave you) more..." Grey said leaning against the footboard again.

I sat back down with the fresh glass.

"Please help me, Grey. What's wrong with me? What's up with Rune?"

"I don't know what's wrong with you; but I will get to the bottom of it. I can tell you the rest; the parts I know (the rest I'll find out for you)." Grey said solemnly, pushing away from the footboard to fold his arms over his chest.

Grey looked like the majority of Middle Eastern men except he was really more spectacular.

I listened (or waited to listen) clearing my thoughts especially the negative ones.

159

Just listen, Jinx. Hear every word Grey says and don't try to read into it. Let him interpret and you ask questions, my conscience told me.

"Rune Kalakos is the son of a love Jinn protector. His father was a strong protector; but he had a fault...Semadar. I wish you could see a picture of her...a painting. She was sweet and innocent (so she seemed). Personally I think this was her way of bewitching men. Anyway Rune's father had Rune as an out. He trained Rune to take his place and avoid succumbing to Semadar. He hid Semadar's lamp, gave her charge to Rune and married Rune's mother." Grey said pausing here for my benefit.

"So that part is true." I said with an understanding nod.

"Yes that's true. I knew Rune as a protector and he was great. He knew his limits and he knew the rules. Of course he probably didn't know what Semadar was capable of. The Council more than likely did. And they probably told him much later after he had changed places with Semadar. I can only guess it pissed him off a lot. They probably sent word through his protector but by then Rune was committed." Grey nodded as well, studying my facial expressions.

"His protector is Conrad. Do you know him?" I asked.

Grey smirked. "Whiney Greek. Yeah I know Conrad."

"Do you know what happened to Semadar?"

"I believe she became a different Jinn. I can find out if you really want to know." Grey shrugged.

"I want to know that and why Rune is or was against me being a Jinn." I said feeling that negativity creep in.

"After Semadar female love Jinn started disappearing. And a lot of male love Jinn were frightened that females would grow too strong especially with weak protectors. Rune might have been one of them; but he wouldn't know who the Council would chose as your protector. But you would have to understand his negative opinion. I do." Grey explained sounding oh-so-sensible. And I believed him?

"That was long before me..." I started to say.

"There are some who still feel that way. And there's nothing saying that as a former protector that Rune wouldn't know that the first Jinx would evolve into a female love Jinn. There's also no way of knowing (without going to the Council) how long ago Rune expressed his opinion about you." Grey said expressing doubt in Sigyn's words.

"Or I could ask him...But I just think he'll just lie." I huffed sipping more wine.

"Rune has always been honorable. Yes he's a former protector so he could be prone to telling you what you need to know when you need it. But I don't think Rune is our problem." Grey said making a lot of sense.

I didn't want to address any other problems right now. I wanted to know if I could trust Rune and his feelings or not.

"Go see what you can find out about Rune since Semadar." I said flatly, dismissively.

Knock, knock.

"Jinx, Kyle's here. He's got sushi and some ideas for the new office." Violet said into the door.

"New office?" Grey uttered.

"Don't ask." I mumbled removing the soundproofing.

TWENTY-TWO

Even after Grey tried to talk me off of the ledge and Violet's encouragement I still didn't want to trust Rune.

When he called after sushi and briefly introduced himself to Violet and Kyle I was fuming. They were loving him; which made me even more mad.

"OK. Enough with Violet and Kyle! We need to talk!" I declared abruptly, snatching the phone away from Violet.

Violet, Kyle and Rune gasped as I stormed from the kitchen table into my room. I slammed the door shut, ready to give him an earful.

Before I could say another word the phone was snatched from my hand. I spun around thinking I'd find Grey. Instead I found Rune. Eek!

I was big and bad Jinx over the phone. That was before I thought Rune would show up on me.

"Where is the woman I first met?" Rune asked me between me and the bedroom door.

"You mean the one that you knew everything about before I showed up at your studio?" I quipped finding my voice suddenly (even though it was a nasty one).

163

Rune tossed my phone on my bed, showing a little bit of frustration.

"I already told you I saw you get out of the car. Where's this coming from?" he remarked.

"Just admit it. All you've done is lie to me." I snapped.

Rune rubbed his temples again.

"Watch what you say because I'm having you checked out too." I added with an arrogant smirk. This so wasn't me. What was happening to me?

"Who's checking me out?" he asked stepping closer to me. I suddenly didn't feel so cocky again.

I think I was becoming bipolar.

"Grey." I stated shakily.

"Grey Alavi or whatever his last name is this century?" Rune asked seriously. I nodded.

"So they did give the best protector for you through time," he added looking a little relieved.

"I told you my protector's name and you pretended not to know it. Is there anything that was the truth?" I said, anger raising its ugly head again.

"What did he tell you? I'm sure Grey didn't need to go in front of the Council for me. We knew each other when I was a protector. He knew my father too." Rune said folding his arms over his chest.

"He said that...that you knew each other. He also said that you might have been set up for failure by your father because he had a history with Semadar; but you didn't know this until you

164

had switched places with her. Well that's what Grey assumed. He also said that no one was liking female love Jinns..."

"I'll stop you right there so you can hear me out." Rune interrupted me seriously.

"Will you still be lying?" I asked showing some weakness.

"If I am you can leave me. OK?" Rune said looking me straight in the eyes.

"Deal."

"I was Shang hai'd from the get-go. All I could do was make the best of the situation after Conrad let it slip that the Council was hoping someone would fail with Semadar. The Council didn't want to lose another love Jinn so gaining me was a plus for them. Conrad also let it slip that eventually the newly enslaved man-slave Jinx would become a female love Jinn. I was scared to death for any protectors because I had been one. I thought you would be like Semadar and the remaining females," he explained pulling me to sit next to him on the bed.

"But you were against me...what were you going to do with me once we met?" I asked letting my hand stay in his.

"I never expected to meet you. Like I told you I haven't seen another love Jinn in a long time. I went to the Council about you hoping I could become your protector and make sure you wouldn't be like the others. They shut me down telling me that you had a good protector and I was sent back to my life as a love Jinn. Then I met you and fell in love. I never wanted to bring my past prejudices into our relationship. However I had plans to tell you the truth later but now it's all out there. I have nothing else." Rune expelled softly, stroking a stray hair from my face.

"That's the truth." Grey said out of the blue.

He materialized behind us in the bathroom doorway, startling us. We both stood up to face Grey.

"Good to see that you're well, Rune." Grey added approaching with his right hand extended for a handshake.

They shook hands and Rune stepped back to put his hand on my lower back. A shiver went down my back and I leaned closer to him. Was I trusting him again?

"So everything Rune said was true. The Council confirmed that they used him as a scapegoat with Semadar but they have been delighted with him ever since. Now to Semadar…That's if you're satisfied that Rune and I mean you no harm." Grey affirmed trying to read me.

I put my arm around Rune's waist. "For now I'm going to hang in there."

Rune sighed a little relieved. Grey still looked at me skeptically.

"I'm going to come back to that. But Semadar…The Council does keep record of their losses in case the High Goddess asks. Semadar stopped existing as a love Jinn fifteen years into Alexander's campaign. She became a Jinn of fortune named Nili Sidonie. According to their records she still exists out there somewhere. OK?" Grey replied making eye contact with both of us.

I gazed up at Rune for his reaction. He appeared indifferent.

Grey focused on me solely again.

"When did you start being negative? When did you start to doubt love and trust?"

I shrugged. I couldn't pinpoint it, could I?

"It started (I think) when I couldn't get a hold of Rune when he lost his phone. And it got worse when this chick confronted me in San Diego." I told Grey.

"The female version of Sabretooth, right? Sigyn. She sold me a camera lens and then started harassing Jinx." Rune added, holding me closer.

"She looked like Sabretooth?" Grey puzzled.

"She had huge lower canines with purplish-black hair." I clarified with a little smile.

Grey looked like he was taking mental notes.

"I'll look into that. In the meantime stay optimistic." Grey said finally and disappeared.

Rune spent the night just holding me close. In the morning he popped back to Atlanta and I felt a whole lot better about us. Hallelujah!

"Hey you!" Violet greeted me cheerfully, standing in my bedroom doorway thirty minutes after Rune had left.

I waved because I was brushing my teeth.

"Everything OK?" she asked hopefully, coming into my room to sit on my bed (just like she used to. Oh nostalgia!). Damascus was already sitting up there.

"Everything is good for now. How are you?" I said rinsing my toothbrush.

"I'm glad you asked…" Violet smiled, bright-eyed.

Uh oh!

"It's not that bad. Why do you look like that?" she laughed. Once again my face showed everything and no one read it better than Vi.

"I'm scared about what you're about to say." I said checking my reflection to make sure there wasn't any evidence a man spent the night last night. You know like hickeys. Although Rune was very careful about anything like that; but it would be nice to get one now and again.

I glanced behind me in the bathroom mirror to see Rune's towel draped over the glass shower door. OK. There was that. But Vi never came in my bathroom.

I came out, closing the bathroom door partly and finished getting dressed.

"Well tell me what you're thinking I'm going to say. Maybe you're wrong." Violet said patiently, rubbing Damascus's belly.

"You want me to plan your wedding." I said simply.

"Wrong. I want you to plan my honeymoon." Violet said emphatically, giggling at how Damascus' hindleg started twitching.

"What are you doing for a wedding? Vi…" I asked suddenly afraid that they might have eloped. Uncle Ash and Aunt Mattie would freak out if Violet eloped. Then they would be looking like it's my fault.

Not this girl!

"A wedding but I don't want to pay you for that," she responded.

"You think I'd charge you to do your wedding? Seriously?" I huffed completely offended as I tugged on a black long-sleeve T-shirt over my dark denim jeans.

To show how offended I was I stomped past my cousin into my office.

"I can't expect you to do it for free..." Violet added tailing me.

"First of all Uncle Ash would pay for it and I still wouldn't charge him a lot. You're family." I corrected her, unlocking my laptop and picking up the files I had to work.

"You're telling me that you gave up on taking out Kyle during the service?" she said taking a seat on the loveseat.

How did she know that? I never told anyone about that.

"The look on your face said it all. Tell me that no assassins will show up and I'll consider having you do more than the honeymoon." Violet eyed me.

"I don't know any assassins right offhand. I also don't know any Al Qaeda or Taliban members. But that's OK. I'll do the honeymoon." I said stiffly, getting up to get a bottle of water for my Keurig. I also grabbed a clean glass for my tea.

"Good! I'll let you know when we have a date!" Violet said emphatically as someone knocked on the front door.

I could make out a shadow through the blinds since my office faced the front walk.

"Oh! This should be the Office Depot guy. Did you know they did office set-up planning?" Violet beamed hurrying away.

I rolled my eyes. She was sure gung ho about this joint office thing. Leave her to it, my conscience said. Besides I was busy with ten plus weddings.

TWENTY-THREE

We have a Scottish castle wedding in mind. We've thought about it since you first met with us. What do you think?" Caribe Stephens said to me in our second Skype appointment on Valentine's Day.

I didn't know it was Valentine's Day when I woke up. Violet made it known by running around our new office looking for a special earring. Then she kept neurotically calling the florist to make sure the delivery was on its way. Once she was sure the flowers were en route she neurotically called the Edible Arrangements store to check on *that* delivery.

Before I got on my Skype call with Caribe in Binghampton, England I asked her what the deal was. I should have known though since Violet ran around like this last year...

"Valentine's Day! You should get something for Rune! Do you need ideas?" Violet piped anxiously from her desk facing the backyard.

Our new office was all right and it was better than I expected. The loveseat was dragged under the breakfast bar and Damascus sat there happily watching us. And my old office was empty now.

But it stayed quiet and there was lots more light to bounce off of our glass and metal desks that Violet chose. She even decided to purchase these thirty-two inch Mac monitors to plug our laptops into. Which means this Skype with Caribe was like watching TV.

I had told Violet 'no thank you' and started my call.

"Scottish castle, huh? Did you two decide on a date so I know what we're looking like?" I asked thoughtfully, making notes inside of Caribe and Danielle's folder.

"Well Danielle doesn't like the heat and Scotland can get pretty muggy. I'm thinking in the autumn. I'll get her to narrow the date down." Caribe responded scratching his beard. He almost reminded me of Snoop Dogg (or whatever he's calling himself nowadays).

"I should be out there again in a few weeks. I have some other clients I'm meeting with. Will Dani be home in March?" I smiled to show encouragement. Poor Caribe was trying to plan this wedding all by himself to keep his Posh Spice looking fiancée from stressing out.

"She starts her shore duty in March mat'of fact (that's exactly how he said it)." Caribe smiled back.

"Awesome. I'll let you know when I'm there and the three of us can meet. In the meantime I'll select some open castles that we can tour while I'm there." I said making notes in their file and on my Outlook calendar.

We ended the call and Caribe told me 'Happy Valentine's Day'. I told him the same and demanded that he try to call Danielle on her base in Iceland.

Then it was on to the next call while Violet announced that her sterling silver dolphin earring had been found.

"Crisis averted!" Violet called from her bedroom.

"Lovely!" I called back scheduling cake tasting appointments for Billy and Tamara (we had to reschedule because one of the daughters was sick). I really loved the ability to pop in and out of places (when Violet wasn't looking).

Violet went into the kitchen to pour dog kibble into Damascus' bowl. Damascus' ears pricked up. I glanced at the clock on the monitor to see it was a little after four. Boy! The day just flew by; which was good.

"Got a date?" I asked the obvious question. Of course she had a date...duh!

"Yep! I had to wear my first gift he ever gave me. Isn't that romantic?" Violet beamed setting the bowl down on Damascus' placemat.

"I suppose he's got your gift on him?" I asked hopefully. I really was hoping too because I did want this engagement to go well. Besides maybe this was the answer to my wish for Vi.

"He said it will be awesome!" she squealed taking Damascus' seat on the loveseat.

I smiled, not having anything else to say. I really didn't want to hate. I'd never celebrated Valentine's Day. Other than...well other than never. We didn't do Valentine's Day in Cairo where I attended primary school. Then in high school I never had a boyfriend to send any candy grams too. Once again oh well!

"We're spending the night at Casa Marina and that's just the first part of the gift." Violet continued just as her cell phone rang.

She answered it while she let Damascus out in the backyard. It was Kyle and I kept working.

Twenty minutes later Kyle was at the door to sweep her away, leaving Damascus and me.

I ended my work day to make a date with a fresh bottle of Moscato and Damascus. Damascus decided that we should watch The Avengers after my shower so we did.

I called Rune earlier on my brief lunch break to the post office. He didn't sound too hot but he promised to either call tonight or come by.

So my Valentine's Day evening was spent watching a bunch of hot men (and alright Scarlett Johansson was pretty badass too) with my dream dog and a bottle of wine. We were having a great time too. The Hulk would growl and Damascus would growl.

Then Grey showed up (and I do mean showed up).

"Don't you have a valentine to annoy?" I remarked and then giggled. I might have been a little buzzed since Damascus didn't provide me with dinner. Then again I was really waiting on Rune before I got dinner.

"No. I've never had a valentine. Why? Am I interrupting something?" Grey replied glancing into my bedroom.

Damascus looked from Grey to me and actually shook his head.

I cut my eyes at both of them on the couch, placing the movie on pause.

"Is your cousin coming back soon?" Grey asked next, leaning forward.

I laughed for two reasons: one was because his question sounded like one a guy would ask before he attacked. Two was -

"As mentioned on several occasions I don't need Violet to protect me. I have Damascus."

"Very funny. Last time even *he* was taken." Grey quipped.

Touché!

"Never mind. I didn't come here about that. I have other news." Grey said brushing off any possible argument.

"I hope it's not about Semadar again." I huffed, considering getting up and then I looked over the couch to the kitchen counter. From that distance I spied the empty bottle of Moscato (the bottle I started).

"No. Remember I told you that I'd use my resources to find out about Mrs. Sabretooth? Well I have news. Do you want to hear it or not?" Grey asked with his own huff.

"That was two weeks ago. I've been very busy." I laughed.

"I've been busy too. With my job and this." Grey smirked getting up to go into the kitchen.

He picked up the empty wine bottle and shook his head.

175

"Fine. Go ahead and tell me. Although I think Mrs. Sabretooth has moved on…" I conceded willing myself to stand. Stand and lean against the living room couch.

"Unfortunately for you two she's been waiting a long time and she'd wait a little longer." Grey scoffed, peering into my fridge for a bottle of water. He probably took stock of Kyle's protein shakes and his chilled bottle of Jägermeister. Or at least I hoped he though they were Kyle's (I don't know why).

"What's that supposed to mean?" I asked casually, feeling not so lightheaded.

Grey opened the bottle, took a sip and leaned against the kitchen entrance. He didn't even glance over at my new office. But why would he? He'd never shown interest in my work anyway.

"Mrs. Sabretooth is not just a random crazy woman."

"No?"

"Sigyn was the name of the Norse god Loki's wife. There's no back story or other story about Sigyn other than her being the mother of one of Loki's sons and comforting Loki as he laid dying of snake venom." Grey began carefully sipping his water while he studied me.

"So she's a Norse goddess?" I asked mildly interested.

Grey shook his head.

"Can you just let me tell the story?"

I rolled my eyes and proceeded to get a bottle of water for myself. My silence was Grey's cue to continue.

"So Sigyn was a goddess of no origin or purpose; which is kind of weird. I had to ask every protector I've ever known if they knew more about Sigyn and if it would be an unusual name to give a child. I got back two separate tales. Ready?" Grey continued while I drank my water and opened the cabinet next to the fridge.

The top shelf of the cabinet next to the fridge held my treats-dark chocolate. I needed something in my stomach and I didn't feel like wishing for something.

"Ready." I smiled triumphantly, pulling a bar of chocolate down from the shelf.

"The first tale told to me was that Sigyn was never a goddess of no origin. Loki's wife was a peace offering from the Norse gods to Dark Elfs or rather *between* Norse gods and Dark Elfs. Their union was supposed to solidify the peace and the son born to them did that. But when Loki's sentenced to die Sigyn doesn't return to her homeland like she was supposed to do. And there's also no one to mind their son. Sigyn's father came to her while she was emptying the bowl of venom. He told her that her place was with her son and the alliance had run its course. So with that Sigyn left Loki's side to be with her son to raise him as a god. That tale ends with her seeing many descendants before she died at the ripe age of four hundred and two." Grey regaled me.

All I could see were the creepy Dark Elfs from the second Thor. I didn't see any female Dark Elfs in that movie so I was surprised to think of any creepy female Elfs. Well other than Sigyn.

"Damn Tom Hiddleston." I retorted snapping my fingers in disappointment. I had long since finished the chocolate.

Grey shook his head again. Damascus trotted in to survey the scene and then he went to my room probably to go to bed.

"The second tale comes from another protector whose love Jinn is in Russia. It picks up in the recent past. How much did you read from your grandfather's letters?" Grey asked deciding that this could be a conversation now.

"All of them. I had a lot of time on my hands while stuck in that lamp. Why?" I answered with a yawn. It had been a long day.

"Did you read anything about him slighting someone in 1950?" Grey asked probably out of curiosity, drinking more of his water.

I thought back and because I wasn't sure I went into my bedroom to pull the journal out of its hiding place. The journal was the last thing Gramma Nasira gave me (then she keeled over on my couch last July). In the journal were life lessons and letters. The letters were mostly from my grandfather who didn't really do what he was supposed to do as a love Jinn.

I flipped through the letters for a postmark from 1950.

"1950 exactly?" I asked curiously, glancing up at Grey in my bedroom doorway.

"The protector said that a request went out to appease an ancient evil with pure love. Everyone ignored it until the only one who was left who hadn't ignored it was your grandfather." Grey told me probably hoping it would help me.

There wasn't anything in the letters. There wasn't anything in the journal as I sat down on my bed to go page by page.

After thirty minutes I still didn't find anything.

"You might as well tell me the rest. Grandpa was Grandpa; more absorbed in his own love life." I sighed with another yawn.

"Sigyn found your grandfather. She came to him as a normal looking human between Nasira and the previous lover. She knew he was a love Jinn. At first she tried to get him to help her. She tried a ton of ways to induce him to find love for her. But your grandfather seduced her and even made love to her on the eve of being on that train where he met Nasira. When Sigyn revealed her true self he scorned her and asked me to help remove her memory of him so he could feel pure. It was all messed up." Grey explained awkwardly and I could see why.

I groaned and fell back on my bed. I saw it all clearly now.

"One! Did my grandfather have a first name? Two! Did he do anything that wasn't about himself? Three! Did you advise him at all?" I shouted in aggravation. Damascus stirred and went into my bathroom to hide.

"Of course he had a first name: Khourshed. And he thought having a legacy was more important. His plan lead to you which I didn't think about. Like I said I thought when he died I would die so we were about living life." Grey said in their defense.

"But now this chick is after me, right? Did your comrade tell you that?" I snapped sitting up abruptly.

Grey made this seesaw motion with his free hand.

"It's not more or less, Grey. Tell me the truth please." I said a little more calm once I heard my voice.

"OK. She's out to get you and we don't know where she is." Grey admitted.

"But she will come back to make sure I'm as unhappy as she is...She's probably why I lost Andrea..." I huffed suddenly really sad.

"No I checked on that. Apparently Sigyn was asleep until Rune decided to go to the Council about you. She knew about your grandfather's line when she fell asleep..." Grey said with a wince. The wince and the lack of confidence was new on Grey.

"I wasn't even born. She shouldn't know about me." I stated.

"I don't know how she knew you were the Jinn. She knew it when she heard it though. How she heard it in Council I really don't want to know." Grey replied just as his cell phone rang.

He answered it all official-like so it had to be the Sheriff's Office calling.

"I've got to go now." Grey said when he put his phone back in his pocket.

I waved him off and before I could worry about Sigyn anymore I passed out.

But while I was asleep I knew exactly how Sigyn was going to make me really miserable. Rune!

My eyes flew open. I rolled out of my bed on Rune's side to fling my closet door open. It was going to be cold in Atlanta so I needed to dress like it.

Ten minutes later I shoved my toothbrush back its holder and gave Damascus a kiss bye. I sent a text to Violet to let her know that an emergency came up and Damascus was by himself.

"Auntie Vi will be back soon. I have to check on Mr. Rune." I told Damascus as I checked his water bowl. I refilled it and found a treat for Damascus.

I gave it to Damascus and wished to be where Rune was. Then I popped out of Jacksonville to Atlanta.

Where I appeared was not where I expected.

I looked around me to see cop cars coming and going from the lot. Did I think Grey instead of Rune and end up at one of the police substations in Jacksonville?

Nope. I was in Atlanta. The sides of the police cars said Atlanta Police Department. Dial 911.

"Why am I here?" I asked out loud moving out of the way for a pissed off woman cursing a beat-up man. Bar fight bailout.

"This is just plain crazy, Rune. Don't you think? They can't hold you responsible for that," a feminine and Southern voice said almost on top of me.

"Watch out, Jill!" Rune called out before his assistant bumped into me accidentally.

181

"Rune! Jill!" I exclaimed in return.

They both stopped and gawked at me.

"You must have checked your messages." Rune said hastily, wrapping his arms around me.

"Yes and I probably drove faster than I should have to get here. I was so worried." I added kissing him on the cheek.

"Oh! So you're going to be OK with Jinx?" Jill asked with a big yawn.

"I'll be fine. Thanks Jill for bringing the bail money." Rune smiled forcefully at his assistant.

Jill smiled and patiently bailed out.

"We'll catch the bus. Go on home." Rune said ushering Jill away.

Sure. The bus. Whatever.

Jill went to her car and got in.

"You know I just said I drove here and you said we'll take the bus..." I whispered to him while I smiled and waved.

"I don't lie too well under pressure. Maybe you should wish your car here then." Rune suggested.

"No. We're just not on our game because I left a message that I was leaving on an emergency but my car is in the garage." I groaned popping myself in the forehead.

Rune took my hand and started leading me towards a car that looked like my Altima. As we got closer I realized it was my car. It was the only slate gray Altima with Duval County plates (I hadn't gotten around to memorizing the plate number yet).

We got in and miraculously the key was in the tri-cup holder (without the keys we wouldn't be going anywhere). I glanced over at Rune, whose head was against the passenger side window, knowing he had made this possible.

I hit the Start button, pulled out of the spot and drove to Rune's townhouse. I waited for him to say something. I mean seriously. I just ran into my boyfriend (he was still my boyfriend, right?) at a police substation in Atlanta after he was bailed out by his assistant.

The sun was just beginning to rise as I pulled up in front of Rune's neighbor's again.

We got out and Rune let us in while I set my car alarm. He locked up, took my hands again and lead us up to his bedroom.

Rune got undressed, took a shower and then came back into the room dressed for bed. I sat on the edge of the bed numbly.

I came here so gung ho to save him and us from Sigyn but now...I wasn't so sure.

He scooted me over and laid down staring up at the ceiling.

The silence was killing me.

"You didn't want me here..." I said shakily, gazing down at my lap. If I looked at him I would cry (I knew it).

"I'm glad you did come," he said in Greek.

"Are we still together?" I asked next looking at his immaculate feet now.

"Of course. You think I'm mad at you?" Rune said tugging the sleeve of my sweater so I would look at him.

"We haven't been real warm and cheery lately." I noted glancing at him over my shoulder.

"I have a feeling you came here with some resolution." Rune said.

"I didn't expect to find you at the police department though. It kinda put what I had to say on the back burner." I sighed, turning around completely to sit cross-legged next to him.

Rune rubbed his temples.

"I was arrested for attempted murder of an infant I photo-graphed on New Year's Eve. They have a little bit of evidence or circumstantial evidence; but I still feel responsible. Jill brought my money to bail me out."

I suddenly saw the baby he mentioned in my memory. Her negatives looked weird too. But dead? The baby was dead?

"What are you going to do?" I asked anxiously, taking his left hand from his temple to hold.

"What I normally do when there's trouble...move," he responded as if it was obvious.

"What about me? You're just going to up and leave me?" I gasped. Oh no he wasn't!

"Do you have any better ideas?" Rune asked staring at me.

"Matter of fact I do. I was hoping to head this off at the pass; but I guess I'm late. Have you given up?" I stated confidently, holding his hand tighter.

The tired worried look on Rune's face disappeared and transformed into a sly grin.

"Talk to me."

"Grey came to me earlier last night to tell me who Sigyn was. Apparently she's someone who wanted to find love and all of the love Jinns ignored her. The only one who partially entertained her was my stupid grandfather. But he turned her away after she fell in love with him. So she's out for vengeance against me." I began to explain.

"Sigyn Pikoos? Of course!" Rune exclaimed sitting upright.

"You remember her?" I gasped. Duh! He's been a love Jinn a long time. He would have existed in 1950 with Grandpa.

"I've been so stupid! Sigyn Pikoos did come to me to find love! I lived in Canada to avoid being drafted into any wars back then!" Rune actually laughed, standing up beside the bed.

I gaped at him. He was probably laughing for several reasons. Number one might have been sleep depravation delusion. I'm going with that one.

"It was late 1948 when I found her on my doorstep. She seemed to know exactly who I was; but I had no clue what she was. She scared the crap out of me and Conrad warned me against helping her. So I listened to him and told her that I didn't do that work anymore. Then I never saw her again." Rune recalled and I could see life in his blue eyes again.

"Well she's a Dark Elf, Rune. A pissed off one. She's been asleep until you went to the Council about me. Then she must have known something else because she's determined that I not find love; probably especially with you. Another love Jinn who spurned her." I explained feeling a little giddy at his craziness.

"Dark Elf? No wonder Conrad told me to leave her alone. I have never did well with immortal creatures." Rune remarked sitting down on the bed again.

"Yeah well I think I have a plan to get Sigyn off our butts." I sighed realizing that Rune was still throwing up his hands of all of this.

"Is it going to keep me from going to jail?" he asked curiously, studying me.

"If done right yes. Do you want to hear it?" I answered still feeling optimistic. It was a simple plan but sometimes the best plans were that simple. We just complicate everything.

Rune nodded.

"We're going to find what she was looking for seventy years ago. We're going to research Dark Elfs and find Sigyn true love (or whatever Dark Elfs need)." I smiled glancing from Rune to the full sunrise out of the bedroom window. Another glorious day.

When I gazed back at Rune he looked dumbfounded.

"You can do this, Rune. I know you only do young love and all. But think of it this way. It will be young love for Sigyn. Besides you're just going to be assisting me."

"Assisting you doing what? It's been so long. Man! What if I'm becoming like your grandfather?" Rune said coming down for his previous high.

"I won't allow you to become so self-involved like my grandfather. We're going to right a wrong because I don't turn away anyone that comes to me looking for love." I stated seriously, getting up from the bed full of energy.

I was back! I could feel all the nastiness and anger just disappear the more I thought about my plan.

"But Sigyn didn't come to you..." Rune said hesitantly.

I went to Rune's side and made him lie down. I even covered him up.

"She did seventy years ago. If my grandfather won't honor a request, then as his granddaughter I will." I smiled kissing him on the lips.

Rune's hands went to my hair hanging around us.

"Why?" he asked softly, searching my eyes.

"Because I want to be in love. I want this to work, don't you?" I answered sincerely, kissing him again. I wished that he'd go to sleep so he would wake up ready to work (you know Jinn work).

"So much," he whispered after I pulled away.

Then I heard the soft snort that marked sound sleep for Rune. Now I wished myself home to get started.

TWENTY-FOUR

I wished the car and me to the light at Abess Park and Kernan, hoping I didn't cause an accident by popping in. Well it was early on Sunday so no one was hurrying to church yet hence no accidents. So I headed home realizing that I was home sooner I expected.

I sent a text to Violet telling her crisis averted. I'd see her when she got home. I also sent a text to Rune to tell him to come see when he woke up. I'd think of some excuse to explain his appearance to Kyle and Violet later.

Once I pulled in the garage I grabbed Damascus' leash and asked him if he wanted a walk before breakfast. He decided that post breakfast would be better for him. So I fed him and started tea for myself.

I was so psyched to feel like myself again. Truly myself right down to my optimism – infinite optimism and hope.

After Damascus was done eating, we took our walk and then came back to get to work. I typically worked Sunday through Friday or six days on and one day off. I basically didn't know a normal work week as a small businesswoman.

But this morning I was doing work for my own personal means.

I went through my phone to find two numbers of people I thought could help me. I tried the first number for the first person because I felt like hearing some good news (maybe?).

"This can't be Miss Jinx..." a cheerful voice answered my call in disbelief.

"It sure is. How are you, Edwin?" I smiled knowing that he probably was too.

"Solange and I are doing very well. I've been living in Aucquince. We have our own square there. My family is so happy." Edwin responded.

"You guys didn't move into her family's square?" I asked with a laugh.

Edwin and Solange were my first introductions to Elfs. Edwin came as a referral from Mr. Spencer who was my introduction to vampires. And to think those introductions happened in July – not so long ago.

In Aucquince accepted family lines lived in the same square perhaps a few levels each per square. Accepted families were pure lines (those who didn't breed outside of the Elf bloodline). Solange's family was old and highly respected. Edwin's family hid in plain sight of humans; preferring humans which made them outsiders.

"So now she's on house arrest." Edwin concluded.

Oh no! I zoned out and now I missed what he was saying.

"I think your line cut off after my question I'm afraid." I lied so he'd repeat what he was saying.

"Understandable. I was saying that her square was full but our new Vaskaya square is off of her grandparents. I was also saying that it was a good thing too because Solange is pregnant and on house arrest." Edwin repeated himself genially. He was such a gentleman.

"I thought that's what you said. Are you lonely? How long will she be on house arrest?" I said between smiling and pouting.

It was awesome that Solange was pregnant three months later; but I knew they were probably really sad, separated the way they were.

"I can talk to her through the door at night as long as I don't see her. No kidding. Her sister Kundry put a dressing screen in front of the door and she sits there making sure no rules will be broken. But it's only a few months more. Until then I live up in the guest bungalows. My new cousin in law Huen is in the bungalow next to me. So I'm not too lonely." Edwin laughed jovially.

"I hope you let me come for the birth ritual." I said before I got to the real reason I called.

"Of course. The trust likes you now. They say that you're a special love Jinn." Edwin said emphatically.

"I suppose I am. I *was* calling to see if you would be able to educate me on something I'm not familiar with." I responded modestly as I heard a clang to my left. Damascus was trying to situate his bone and self under Violet's desk. It was a tight squeeze as he grew and the bone hit the metal desk leg.

"Silly boy!" I tutted covering my headset mouthpiece.

"Sure. What is it you need help with? My specialty is finance." Edwin replied.

"Dark Elfs." I stated bluntly, removing my hand from the mouthpiece so he heard me.

"Dark Elf finances? I couldn't really tell you. They have money but I don't know how." Edwin remarked hiding his obvious displeasure.

"I didn't mean to upset you. I just thought I'd ask you since you entertained my ridiculous questions about Elfs when we first met." I apologized quickly, scrolling in my contacts for the next number.

"You didn't upset me, Miss Jinx. Just caught me off-guard." Edwin said maintaining niceties.

"I don't think you want to hear my crazy notions on Dark Elfs. I don't know enough about them other than low level Elfs and those not in the know pretend they don't exist. Or we grow up hearing scary tales about them so we grow up to be good Elf citizens," he added with a dry laugh.

I laughed so I didn't feel so stupid. But I was still optimistic that I'd find answers somewhere.

"However if you really want to know I can give you Arabella's number. She'd be able to answer your questions within reason." Edwin added in conclusion.

"That would be great, Edwin. Don't forget me for the ceremony now." I said ready to take down Arabella's phone number.

Edwin gave me the same number that Arabella gave me when she took me to the hotel after Edwin and Solange's wedding. Then he told me to keep my schedule open for June and July. I said I would, hoping against hope that I wouldn't have a lot of summer weddings. I really wanted to attend another Elf version of a baby shower.

I checked my clock to see what time it would be in Russia. Oh hell! Russia had six different time zones and I had no idea where this other Elf city was in the country. It was nine-fifteen in the morning in Jacksonville. Russia was either six hours ahead or sixteen hours ahead. Ugh!

So I just dialed and waited.

"T'el residence..." a voice piped on the other end.

"Uh...may I speak with Arabella T'el?" I uttered really praying I wasn't waking anyone up.

"This is Arabella..." the female responded with uncertainty.

"Hey it's Jinx Heydan..."

"Hey Jinx! Why are you speaking in Russian? I don't mind by all means but...How are you? Have you heard that Solange and Edwin are expecting?" Arabella gushed interrupting my awkward said introduction.

Suddenly I felt like an old family friend. Yay!

"Yeah I just heard. I told Edwin I expect to be invited to the ceremony. Is it really early in the day where you are?" I said with a smile.

"It is a little past one in the morning. Why?" she replied still upbeat.

One in the morning?

"I didn't mean to wake you up." I said timidly. I would be pissed if someone woke me up at one in the morning. I wish someone would; that wasn't expected in my bed or anything.

"Don't be ridiculous, Jinx. The baby has yet to sleep through the night. Just when she got used to the early darkness she's now trying to make sense of all of this daylight. We're way out here in the wilderness of Russia you know." Arabella scoffed.

I relaxed a little, getting up from my desk to re-heat my chai tea.

With my breakfast re-heated I sat back down at my desk.

"I just had a general question for you. Edwin said you could help me." I said trying to sound humble and understanding of her plight with baby Narkissa.

Arabella said sure, go ahead.

"Do you know anything about Dark Elfs?" I asked gently just in case I scared her.

"Loads. Tons. Do you have a specific question?" Arabella blurted out.

"Well yeah. What are they and how do their relationships work?" I asked the questions that I needed. After I got my answers I would know what I was up against.

"Dark Elfs and Light Elfs were once a part of the same family. A king and queen, brother and sister. Brother wanted to keep the line pure and away from mortals. He practiced magic that was of the earth. His sister was dark, wanting the line pure and to eradicate mortals. A mortal had tried to seduce her. She killed him and made him her pet. Her magic was dark and eventually she retired to a fortress she built in the mines of Scandinavia. Her brother moved him and his supporters to lighter, brighter places. He was afraid she would be able to get to him if he stayed in the original fortress." Arabella recounted melodically.

I saw the siblings in my mind's eye.

"Do they still exist in those mines?" I asked.

"Some do. Most recently they've been found out here in Russia playing in the shadows." Arabella answered simply.

"Hence why there is an Elfin community in Russia that you and Fox guard." I added catching on.

"Also because our king lives here in Chaepevic. He still fears what his ancestor fears. Why he moved out here no one knows. Oh wait! His queen is from around here. We're still not sure if she can be trusted. Dark Elfs cannot be trusted and always use their magic while we have stopped. Or only a few use it." Arabella said. I could hear the baby babbling close by.

I made notes. "Would Mor be a Dark Elf?"

"She's pretty close. That's why they exiled her even though she's still close to Aucquince. Now what was your other question?" Arabella answered probably rocking her baby girl in her arms.

"Do you know anything about their relationship habits? By the way how do you know all of this?" I asked opening a template I made for matchmaking. I completed the Excel template, sent it to Durward, my web site developer (and former lover and classmate at the community college) and he would put it on the dating portion of Eden's site.

This was all a part of my plan.

"When you become one of the guard they school you on all of the obstacles and adversaries. So I know everything about Dark Elfs – my specialty as Fox would say." Arabella laughed again.

I laughed too, imagining that Fox would have teased Arabella's knowledge. He was probably very lucky to have Arabella while he was in Chaepevic. Edwin did say they were well matched. I used the example of Beyoncé and Jay-Z because they were like a power couple too.

"So relationship habits? Have you been contacted by a Dark Elf, Miss Jinx?" Arabella quickly picked up once she was given a moment to think properly.

Might as well tell her the truth...maybe?

"Well I was watching Thor: The Dark World. It's one of my favorite movies. And I got to wondering if Dark Elfs were real since I knew other Elfs were. I just didn't want to wake you up to ask that." Of course I wouldn't tell her about Sigyn. What if Arabella took it upon herself to hunt Sigyn down?

"It's always good to satisfy one's curiosity right away. Ever see those people that wreck their brains out to answer a question that's on the tip of their tongue? Silliness. So you want to know their relationship habits? All right!" Arabella laughed some more.

"Yeah. There's no reason to rack my brains." I chuckled along with her.

"Well Dark Elfs are a little weird. While we use our trust to affirm our choice in partners they don't. They look for like bloodlines. Then they duel until submission with a weapon of choice. I always wanted to see it done...the duel." Arabella said with an air of admiration.

I would have indulged her dark fantasy (because my dork fantasy was to meet Legolas. Not Orlando Bloom. Legolas) but I was stuck on the first part.

"Like bloodlines? Does that mean a relative?" I squeaked out.

"You sound squeamish, Miss Jinx."

"I'm kinda grossed out by the idea of marrying a family member. Don't they worry about inbreeding?" I uttered gulping down the throw-up that was coming up my throat.

Just then me and Damascus heard a key in the front door lock. Violet.

I glanced at the clock. Twenty til ten. Is that early to be back from a Valentine's Day night?

"No they don't. All fertilized eggs are taken from the mother and nurtured by the Elders. Depending on the partnership the Elders will give the baby back. Of course I've heard of situations when the parents get back the number of babies they gave but the babies don't necessarily belong to the parents. It's kind of like a force placed foster system." Arabella continued sounding quite sensible.

Violet and Kyle came into the house laughing and having a good time.

"So it might not be inbreeding if you marry your brother because it might not be your biological brother." I resolved perking up a little.

"Remember they're looking for a like bloodline so if your brother's blood is different you'd keep it moving. And they don't care about the generation. If they meet their biological grandfather a female Dark Elf would challenge him to a duel. Whomever wins the duel is always the dominate party. Some duels end up in death because neither wants to be the submissive party." Arabella threw some wrenches into my just painted pretty picture.

Before I could say anything else there was a very angry wail from Narkissa and Arabella said she had to go. I thanked her for her time and silently promised to get a picture of a real Dark Elf duel for her. Then we hung up.

I filled in the template as if I was Sigyn and sent it over to Durward. In the email I told Durward to upload the template in Cyrillic and English. I wasn't sure what language would get the best results. Elfish would have probably scored immediately but Durward didn't have Elfish script to use for his programming.

"How was your evening?" Violet asked me after they got settled in. I was doing other work then.

"I got another matchmaking client. I'm going to need your help with it though." I said jotting down castles in Scotland for Caribe and Daniella.

"Sure. You're going to London on Monday." Violet smiled from her desk which Damascus had vacated for other parts.

I reached into my in-box and pulled out the file I had started for Sigyn. I gave it to Violet.

"Yep. I'll be gone all week. Sigyn is a repeat client or handle her like one. Matter of fact treat her like Mr. Parisi." I said seriously, spotting a new email drop into my business email.

The email was from my Korean matchmaking client Ha-Neul. I read it and the email contained some of the ideas she had for a May wedding. She wanted to be married before the baby was born.

I responded to the email.

"Mr. Parisi could only be handled by you. What if this woman gets nasty?" Violet remarked perusing Sigyn's file. If she read the part about Sigyn being a Dark Elf she didn't react.

Ding-dong!

Bark! Grrr...

"I'll get it!" Kyle called strolling by with a laundry hamper on his way to the washing machine in the garage.

The rest of us waited to find out who our guest was.

We listened (well I listened because I didn't have a line of sight to the front door) and I heard Rune's voice first.

I jumped out of my seat to rush to him; but Damascus tried to trip me up en route. I could swear Damascus was jealous of me and Rune. Either that or he saw me as a rival.

"You have to love the daily flights from Atlanta to Jacksonville." Rune said, giving me a big hug like he hadn't seen me in days, weeks.

"Baby, you should have called and I would have picked you up." I beamed so glad to see him looking more like himself.

"It's OK. I caught a ride with a nice elderly couple that sat beside me on the plane. They tried to hook me up with their granddaughter who has four kids. I politely declined since I was here to see my girlfriend as a surprise." Rune smiled and came up with this little tale for Kyle and Violet's benefit. I knew full well how Rune got here.

"That's a dangerous thing to do. What if they were murderers or looking for sex slaves? We're real big on sex slaves here in Jacksonville. Right, Kyle?" Violet gasped leaning against the archway into our office. That's as far as she could stumble before her knees would give out.

Kyle added to his fiancée's remark while Violet gestured that she needed me. I caught the flag down out of the corner of my eyes. I could only guess what she was about to say.

"Is that the hot soccer player?" Violet hissed into my ear.

Hot soccer player? Remember I follow soccer (or football as the rest of the world called it). We love soccer in Iran. But who was she thinking was a footballer?

I glanced back at Rune who was taking Kyle's chiding with good spirits.

"Rune?" I asked looking back at Vi.

"That's not your new sweetie Rune. That guy looks like Christiano Ronaldo with longer hair.

God! If he had longer hair the women would really be climbing the walls." Vi remarked with her light eyes fixed on Rune. Vi had hazelish green eyes from her Egyptian mom Aunt Mattie.

I rolled my eyes, turning away from my crazy cousin.

"Rune, this is my cousin Violet Hedayat." I said trying to sound charming and endearing; which was hard because I wanted to be a smart ass.

I knew she was ogling Rune but she ogled Andrea too. Really I couldn't blame her. Every guy I've brought home in the past six or seven months has been beautiful.

"Where do you find such guys, Jinxie?" Violet said beaming brightly to be properly introduced. I loved the dramatic fill-in-the-blank pause she made. Even Kyle rolled his eyes, carrying on with the laundry.

"Atlanta." Rune and I said in unison.

He took Violet's extended hand, shook it and kissed her left cheek.

"You don't sound like you're from the South." Violet remarked and Kyle seconded it.

"I'm not. I've just lived there for ten years. Might I trouble someone for a drink?" Rune replied flashing that beautiful smile I loved.

"Wine! Wine all around!" Violet exclaimed rushing away.

"Vi, it's before noon! Don't give that man wine first thing in the morning!" Kyle scolded his girlfriend.

She yelled that she'd brew some coffee in my Keurig since her coffeemaker was still on a cargo ship.

The rest of us looked relieved.

Rune gave me this look that said 'come here' so I did. He pulled me into him still standing in our two by ten square feet linoleum foyer. He kissed me.

"I got your message after you put me to sleep. That was you, right?" Rune said to me in Greek as Kyle came back from the garage.

"What language is that?" Kyle asked curiously.

"Greek. I'm Greek." Rune said politely, eyeing me.

"Is there a language you don't know?" Kyle scoffed at me. Jealous much?

"Jinx has a talent for languages." Violet piped eagerly, pulling out coffee mugs as the first K-cup finished.

"You don't have to sell me your cousin. I've already purchased with no returns." Rune chuckled in English, taking my hands to lead me into the kitchen.

Violet cooed and ahhed over Rune's little compliment.

Once all of the coffee mugs were filled we sat down in the office; even Kyle.

"So this is Jinx and my office. A lot of people don't know that Eden is a home-based business." Violet felt like she had to say.

"I hear it does well for a small business." Rune commented genially, sipping his black coffee (which I loved knowing that he preferred. I felt like I knew something special).

"What do you do again?" Kyle asked Rune so he was contributing more than his suddenly nutso girlfriend.

"Remember, babe, he told us he was a photographer." Violet chimed in because she just had to say something. She probably felt *she* knew something special. Man!

"But you used to be a matchmaker like me." I added to steer the conversation. Well at least I was trying.

"You don't look old enough to have had two careers." Violet said to Rune from the loveseat.

Damascus had shadowed Rune into the office and even he rolled his black eyes at Violet with his head on Rune's lap. If only I could have been a dog. They hide their expressions real well.

"Don't you have more than one career, Jinx?" Kyle asked behind clenched teeth. He probably wanted to drag Violet out of the room by her hair.

"Yes I do. How keen you are to notice." I remarked cordially, sipping my fresh chai tea.

"Why are you guys acting like that? We have a guest here." Violet asked suddenly (dare I say magically) sounding more like level-headed Vi.

I glanced over at Rune with a sly grin.

"I'm forty-two. I've had time to dabble in different ventures." Rune said.

"I'm her assistant and accountant among other things." Violet said sensibly, drinking her coffee.

"She told me that. Are you private? I'm looking for a new CPA. Jinx can tell you that I'm horrible with bookkeeping. My assistant Jill keeps my schedule straight but my records..." Rune responded engaging my cousin in shop talk.

Twenty minutes later Violet had a new client and she and Kyle had realized that Rune didn't bring any luggage.

I was sitting there searching for one of those crafty swift Jinx responses when Rune replied.

"I have some items here, babe, from my last visit. You said you were kind enough to wash them."

"You've been here before?" Violet croaked out in surprise and then recovered. "It must have been your cologne I smelled in my room then."

Uh no and uh no!

"Let me check on those clothes, baby." I said quickly, hurrying to my bedroom.

I was closing my door to scream when I heard Rune excuse himself. Then he was the one closing the door.

"Grey." Rune said, flipping the lock on the door.

"He stayed here for a bit after Vi left because he felt like he could protect me better." I confessed. Honestly I couldn't remember if I had told Rune that or not.

But now that I think about it. It probably looked real bad now because Grey had appeared in my bedroom when Rune was here like it was nothing.

"He stayed in Violet's room not in here?" Rune asked seriously. His left hand gripped my footboard and his right hand on my dresser, blocking any natural exit. You know in case I wanted to do the human thing and run.

"Of course he slept in Violet's room. He wears too much cologne to stay in here with me for one. For two we're not like that. For three my parents would freak if I was living with a man." I answered calmly, opening a drawer to find Rune's clothes.

Rune's face changed from deadpan to bordering on amused.

"Your cousin doesn't know?"

"No. She can't know. Oh my God and Allah! My aunt and uncle would ship me directly to Karaj if my parents told them to for disobedience." I hissed, closing the drawer loudly in case Kyle and Vi were listening in.

"Yet you spend the night with me?" Rune said now in Greek.

Only two languages were spoken fluently in this house: Arabic and English. We could have spoken in Elfish and Kyle and Vi wouldn't understand.

"I can do that. But if I start to leave stuff at your house, they consider we've moved in." I explained pushing him in his hard chest playfully.

Rune leaned over and kissed me a few times.

"Why did you want me to come see you today? I told Jill the studio would be closed for a few days. To which she replied that she was going to find the next Matlock for me."

"That's sweet of her. Matlock was the best." I smiled.

"Will I need Matlock?" he asked next.

"Not if you help me with my plan." I replied simply, wrapping my arms around his narrow waist.

"You're serious about helping Sigyn?" Rune asked studying my face.

"Yep. The plan is already in motion. I just need for you to help Vi while I'm in the UK. She can monitor the incoming responses if they are in English. Any other language she won't understand. We have to be on point with Sigyn. Vi knows she's priority." I said proudly. Wile E. Coyote you are a genius!

"So you need for me to stay here and man the desk?" Rune asked with uncertainty.

"You can hang out with my crazy cousin if you want. I was just going to give you creative permission with my site and email." I shrugged.

"I'll have an answer for you later. I'm hungry right now." Rune shrugged too, kissing me again.

TWENTY-FIVE

The next morning Rune took us both to the airport. He was going to monitor my site from Atlanta because he was out on bail after all. Me, on the other hand...I had a lot of work to do in England.

"I'll see you tonight." Rune told me seriously, leaving me at my terminal. More than likely he went around the next corner and popped back to Atlanta.

I could have popped to England too but I kinda missed air travel. I always made new friends on flights. Lately I had been meeting men on flights (for instance Chris and Jasper). So I stuck it out and boarded the flight.

And just my luck the economy class was full and I gained a seat in first class. At least I thought it was luck.

"Mimosa, madam?" the sweet Asian flight attendant offered me with a glass in her hand.

"That's extra, isn't it? I don't have a first class ticket." I responded softly so the other passengers didn't sneer at me.

She extended her free hand and I gave her my ticket.

"Mimosa madam. Please lower your tray. We are serving warm croissants or waffles if you prefer," she said handing my ticket back to me.

I lowered my tray a little confused until I looked at my ticket.

First class was circled. I turned it on the reverse in case I missed something.

"If you have to fly, fly like a princess. I love you and will see you tonight, was written on the back in Rune's Greek writing.

I laughed and enjoyed my mimosa and croissants.

After my layover in New York City I sat in the first class again next to a Scottish grandmother. Awesome!

"Would you mind if I ask your opinion on something?" I asked Louisa after she introduced herself.

"Why of course! Make the flight pass quicker. I love the grands but this flight is horribly long." Louisa replied in her brogue. She kinda reminded me of Mrs. Doubtfire.

A horribly long flight but you're sitting in a plush comfy seat in first class. Try sitting with the regular folk in the back.

"I'm a wedding planner and I have a client that I'm meeting in London. They want to get married in a Scottish castle. I looked up a few. Could you give me your honest opinion of them? Maybe suggest a few?" I said brightly, pulling my laptop out since we were all clear for electronics.

"I've never met a wedding planner. Do you do well?" Louisa said just as cheerfully as I was bright.

"I do alright." I said modestly, bringing up my list of prospective venues for Caribe and Daniella.

"Do you have Aldourie on your list?" Louisa asked curiously as I turned my screen in her direction.

I did have the castle on my list. It was one of the priciest if you wanted to book the whole dang thing.

"Just beautiful. I've never had the pleasure to stay there," she added scanning my list further.

"The Mansfield Castle is lovely. I took me grands there when they came on holiday. Just a day trip mind ye. But my personal favorite is Cringletie in Peeblesshire. I don't see it on ye list, darling." Louisa continued.

"Thank you, Louisa!" I beamed, typing the new castle into my list.

While I had my laptop out I researched each castle again and Louisa added little bits before she took a nap. And she stayed asleep until we reached Heathrow where I nudged her.

I thanked her again for her suggestions before I lost track of her. Then I headed to my hotel for the day so I could get ready for tomorrow.

It was a track meet for the next three days; which meant that I was nonstop running (that might not be the right phrase).

I met with Pippa and her brides' maids (the same girls from the convention plus two) at a bridal salon Teohath in the Kingston area of London. I wanted to go to a shop on Walworth in downtown London; but Pippa begged that we go to Kingston. But we left there with the brides' maids dresses picked out which is saying something since we were looking for styles straight out of the twenties.

The day after that and for two days afterward I met with Caribe and Daniella to tour those castles. On the third day I met with them at my hotel restaurant for lunch to discuss what we had seen so far.

"It's so hard to decide." Daniella sighed so overwhelmed. I know I was. The castles were gorgeous.

"I have a list of pros and cons if that will help." I suggested opening my Stephens-McCarrick folder to pull out my wedding venue list.

"Which ones did you like?" Caribe asked me since I was the wedding planner.

"You first." I smiled wanting them to contribute. I had a favorite; but it was for completely different reasons than what a bride and groom would have.

"I was in love with Aldourie. It's exactly what I imagined, Cari." Daniella gushed with stars in her brown eyes.

"If that's what you imagined then that's the one." Caribe said with his arm around her shoulders.

"I couldn't have said it any better. Aldourie it is then. Let me ask a few more questions before I call Albert." I said pleasantly, finding Albert Machalby's business card in my purse. I really needed a business card holder for my purse for new vendors. That was a mental note.

Daniella and Caribe nodded.

"Most importantly did we want to book the whole castle? Albert explained for a little over ten thousand pounds we can have free reign of the castle for a day and night." I asked glancing down at my budget for venue. It definitely wasn't ten thousand pounds.

Daniella blanched at the cost.

"Calm down. The total wedding budget is ten thousand US dollars so the Aldourie is $5,882 US dollars. We still have five thousand to play with. But if we use the Aldourie we have lodging, reception site and wedding venue out of the way." I said calmly, reaching out to pat Daniella's hands on the table.

"Is our budget too high?" she asked next, unaware of the budget since Caribe was handling everything.

"Anything unspent we can always get back, Dani," he said just to pacify her.

We both knew that's not what my contract stated but I was willing to work with them.

We had lunch and I called Albert while I still had my clients available to check on available dates.

"Halloween. Does he have Halloween or November first?" Daniella asked anxiously.

"The first is available. We usually host a ghost tour for tourists on Halloween every year so I can't give you that day." Albert told me hearing Daniella.

"The first it is then. Do you accept outside catering? If yes can you recommend anyone? If not can you provide your menu?" I said taking out my planner to flip to November.

"We have multiple menus to choose from and we are willing to create one specifically for you. I will send you the menus. How do you prefer?" Albert said stiffly, definitely Scottish (most are no-nonsense).

I gave my and Caribe's email addresses to Albert. Then I told Albert that I would be in touch especially to try out the menus.

With that resolved and pinned down my clients were relieved and could move on with their day.

I went back up to my room and packed. Then I was surprised to find Rune at my door ten minutes later.

"You are a busy woman," he remarked taking in my suitcases on the bed.

"Yeah I can't *see* my clients. Sometimes I have to hang out with them. How are you, baby?" I sighed feeling a little guilty seeing him now.

He did come on my first night in London like he promised. But after that I kept finding him asleep in my bed when I came back from treks to Scotland. My poor angel!

"Hanging in there until you can fix this. Jill calls and checks in. I have an appointment to meet with an attorney later today." Rune said falling back on my bed between my suitcases.

Honestly I wanted to straddle him but I had an actual evening flight to Dublin to meet with one of my ten UK couples.

But you're a Jinn you say. I know!

So I straddled him.

"What's going on in Ireland?" Rune asked stroking my arm as I laid naked next to him much later.

"Introductory meeting with Liam and Shawn and then I get to come home." I said lazily, really wanting to stay in his arms all night; but I had to get to Dublin.

"Then I hope it is a quick day and I'll have you in my arms tomorrow morning." Rune said optimistically.

Then Rune wished me dressed and standing outside of the Dublin airport with my bags. Damn Jinn!

TWENTY-SIX

The next morning I woke up with my wake-up call, jumped in the shower and got dressed. I decided to wear my black hair up in a bun with a cream cowl-necked sweater and black slacks with cream pinstriping and my round tip knee length boots. It was cold in England so I knew it would be freezing in Ireland. I even threw on my red thigh length pea coat.

Then out the door I went to find a Starbuck's, Teavana or something. I'd never been to Ireland. Northern Ireland yes. Northern Ireland was still a part of the UK while Ireland was not; which made me excited to see it all. Would I get the chance tough?

I happened to find a Starbuck's on O'Connell Street after I wandered around. I made it inside just as a snowflake landed on my boot. I got a big cup of chai tea and sat in front of the window to marvel at the snowfall.

The snow fell and got all slushy as I called Shawn to ask if they would be willing to meet me at the Starbuck's. I had a rental car but driving in slushy show for a girl that never drove in snow? That would be a not so good idea.

Shawn piped a sure (at least I think she did. Irish is very hard to comprehend when I'm too busy watching people sliding around). She said she call Liam and have him meet us there.

We hung up after I asked her what Liam and her drank so it would be ready for them.

Thirty minutes later I finally got to meet Liam Shanahan. I had already met Shawn at the bridal convention in September. And if I had to compare Shawn Finley to someone it would be Julia Louis-Dreyfus from Seinfeld (even overseas we saw Seinfeld in syndication). She was short, curly haired and vibrant. I couldn't wait to work with her.

"I'm so glad you could come out here and meet us. I didn't think we would be able to meet." Shawn beamed running her hands through her hair after taking off her woolen cap.

Liam was wearing the still fashionable black fedora which allowed for not so fashionable earmuffs. Now Liam reminded me of Fred and George Weasley. He had already shown me that he was witty and a practical joker within ten minutes. He had told Shawn that he had nicked off a portion of his finger at work. Then he showed her his glove missing a finger.

"He just loves messing with me." Shawn had said elbowing her fiancé.

"What do you do, Liam?" I asked after I realized that it was a joke.

I pulled out my notebook where I took my notes (later I put them in the client's file). I liked to take notes on couples that I wasn't responsible for making. I made notes on things like my observations too so I felt like I knew the couple better.

"Mechanic. I love cars. Passion of mine." Liam beamed and then got up to grab some more sugar for his tea.

Shawn chuckled and rolled her brown eyes. "Work on cars night and day if I let him."

"Even if you didn't, love." Liam laughed when he came back. He placed a kiss on her forehead and sat down. "Only thing stopping me is the garage space."

"He'd have us living in a car if it meant he could be close to it." Shawn quipped sipping her mocha Frappuccino despite the weather. I guess I shouldn't judge her since I drink tea every day no matter the weather.

"That's why I have you, baby doll." Liam said nudging her softly.

"Shawn said you two have known each other since primary school. Did you think you would be getting married?" I interjected seeing that these two could possibly go all day whether I was there or not.

Shawn looked at Liam and said, "Tell her."

"I told Shawn in fifth grade that I'd marry her and she gave me the flag if I recall correctly." Liam grinned.

There was something more to the story and I'm sure I'll hear more about it as time goes.

I laughed because it seemed like the right thing to do.

"So since Shawn said yes have you thought of a date?" I asked staying on topic.

"We both are between a short or a long engagement." Shawn answered with a seesaw motion with her hand – the left hand with the cute heart shaped diamond ring. I'd never seen a heart shaped engagement ring before this and I was willing to blog about this tomorrow.

"For two different reasons." Liam added sipping his tea.

I waited to hear the reasons, pen poised.

"Shawn's finishing up her schooling to be a nurse. She's guaranteed a teaching position or a position at the children's hospital. We're not sure if we want to wait for more money next spring or to get married in the winter." Liam explained placing a kiss on Shawn's cheek.

"Basically you're referring to how much you'd be able to spend..." I said so I was clear.

Shawn and Liam shrugged and nodded.

OK. That's sensible.

"But next spring or early this winter though?" I asked before I wrote it down.

"Yes. And we already know we don't want a big wedding." Shawn answered me, stirring her drink with her straw to melt the ice.

"Did you want the small wedding here at home?" I asked writing down 'small wedding'.

"We're waffling on that too. Shawn wants to go away and I want to stay here." Liam shrugged.

"Not a problem. I can work up different scenarios for you based on date, locale and budget." I said cheerfully, making more notes.

"If we get married in the winter our budget is five thousand Euros. If we get married in the spring we can double that. I can possibly sell one of my cars for a winter wedding if the scenarios are favorable." Liam told me and I made note of that too.

"Really Liam? You'd sell one of your babies for our wedding?" Shawn asked her fiancé in surprise.

"That's how you got the ring you wanted. I'd do anything for you, Shawn." Liam blushed to match his red hair.

After that I tied up our first consultation by getting email addresses, good contact times and contact numbers. I gave them my business card and brochure again.

"So we'll hear from you?" Shawn asked just so she was clear.

"Give me two weeks and I shall have a few ideas to send to you two." I smiled confidently, quickly making a reminder for myself on my iPhone app.

Then I gave them each a hug, put my notebook and anything else into my huge Michael Kors purse and I was ready to go. Liam gave Shawn a hug and kiss and went back to work. Shawn went home to study, she said.

I got in my rental car, considering the drive to the hotel.

I looked at the keys in my hand, the ignition and then outside at the pedestrians around me. I swear I saw a squirrel lose his footing and slide headlong into a parked car. I cringed.

"Better idea!" I declared surveying my surroundings before I did some magic. I wished me and the rental car into the hotel garage. Brilliant!

My flight was supposed to leave at six and it was two now. The airport wasn't far away thankfully.

I packed up my bags again, checking my return ticket that Violet bought for me. It would be nice if the return trip was just as cool as the first leg. But that was really Rune's doing not Violet's.

Unfortunately it was a regular economy ticket. Oh well! The people are always chattier in economy seating. Not that Louisa wasn't nice though.

I checked my phone in case Vi or Rune had any hits on Sigyn's match. There was a text from Rune simply saying 'Tonight'. It gave me goosebumps just so you know.

Then I checked out of the hotel, found my rental car in the garage and carefully drove it back to the drop-off point.

"Never drove in the snow, missy?" the cocky black guy garage attendant remarked taking the car keys from me.

"Nope." I admitted. There was no sense in lying about it. My white knuckles couldn't lie or the sweat that beaded on my sunglasses.

"Looks to be the last snow of the year. Maybe you should stay a day or two," he winked. His name badge said his name was Terrell.

"No thank you, Terrell. I'll be back soon enough." I managed to say while I wiped the sweat on my pea coat.

I had changed out of my work clothes into some black denim jeans and a lightweight baby blue and turquoise knit sweater under my pea coat. I put on some sneakers though in case the boot heels tried to kill me.

"I hope sooner than later." Terrell added handing me a receipt as the shuttle bus pulled up on cue.

Terrell motioned to my bags and the shuttle driver clambered out to load them up. I got on the shuttle with a little wave at Terrell.

I got to the airport, checked my bags with the American Airline attendant and then I milled around for lunch or dinner. I still had time to burn (about forty minutes after my life or death drive) and I found a place that had decent Chinese.

I was waiting on my orange chicken when I felt eyes on me. Another uncanny knack of mine. Someone was either watching me on the ground or Grey was watching me like he does; how he does.

My to go order was called and I claimed it. I grabbed some napkins and plasticware hastily. I wanted to get to my terminal as soon as I could.

That's when someone purposely intercepted my path.

"Excuse me." I said at the same time the other person did.

I laughed, stepping around him into Loghan Kerr.

Run!

"Wait!" Loghan and the other person exclaimed in unison. The other person was wearing a hoodie with dark sunglasses. Creepy!

"You and the creepy uni-bomber want me to wait while you rape and kill me?" I quipped. My eyes darted around the area for a quick escape route.

"You are boarding a flight for home, right? It is important we catch you now." Loghan said flatly.

Wrong choice of words, buddy!

"Perhaps better word selection, old man," the person in the hoodie (a man) remarked. At least he had sense.

He pushed back the hood, revealing a thick braid of lemon blonde hair. Dark Elf? Maybe I should have asked what a Dark Elf looked like too.

He didn't remove the sunglasses though.

The man extended his arm for me to take like an escort.

"Loghan, stay here. I'll return for you," he added so I would probably feel more comfortable with him.

Loghan nodded. I swear he looked like he froze standing there. Maybe?

I took the man's arm and he did escort me to my terminal like he knew exactly what flight I was taking. That did make me scared. Loghan was still watching me!

"I apologize if we frightened you. I wanted to catch you as soon as possible. I hope you will not hold that against me," the man said softly in Elfish.

I nodded, not knowing where this talk was going.

"I am Davet. I wanted to answer your call but I only know Elfish and Icelandic. A little English, so little I could not respond. So instead I contacted an old friend Loghan to help. All he could do was have his wife Mor track you," he explained.

Gosh darn it! I knew Elfish would be needed!

"Well you found me, Davet. Although my plane is boarding…" I replied, overhearing a fellow traveler mention the approximate boarding time.

"Yes, *our* plane is boarding. Will I be meeting her when we get there?" Davet nodded sounding nervous. I couldn't see his eyes to confirm whether he was really nervous or not.

I looked back the way we had come like I could still see Loghan standing there.

"Didn't you just tell Loghan you would come back for him?" I reminded Davet.

"So I did." Davet stated bowing his head. Then he raised his head and opened his closed fist.

In his hand looked like a mini replica of Loghan.

My boarding was announced before I could really check out what Davet was holding. So I got in line and Davet got in line behind me. Seriously he was on my flight?

The male flight attendant checked my ticket against my passport, moving me into the terminal. He checked Davet's and moved him along. Was he even looking? This is how terrorists get on flights. Wait! Maybe I shouldn't say that since I'm sure people thought I was a terrorist.

I took my window seat, tucking my carry-on bag under my seat discretely and keeping lunch (or dinner) on my lap until I could bring my tray down.

Davet sat next to me awkwardly.

Once we were in the air I started eating so I wouldn't have to talk. I just didn't know what to make of Davet. He still hadn't removed the sunglasses so I felt like I was sitting next to a blind man.

"Would you like an explanation?" Davet asked switching to Icelandic.

I tossed my napkin into my half empty container, hoping I didn't look disgusted. I was more parched than disgusted. I had to toss my drink at the door of the terminal.

"Yes. I guess I would." I said turning slightly in my seat.

"Since Loghan can be manipulated by magic I can compact him into a miniature. I can do almost anything I want with Loghan. I will return him home when we land." Davet said holding up Loghan again.

Tiny Loghan reminded me of my niece Sumerlin's Polly Pockets. Sumerlin belonged to my brother Taj who was married to an American Rachel. From time to time I'd go over for birthdays or Hanukkah. Taj still lives in Jacksonville somewhere. In August I sent him to Tampa for his wedding anniversary; otherwise we stayed apart.

"And the sunglasses?" I pressed realizing that I couldn't see through the things.

The lights were dim now on the plane because the evening movie was starting. They also kept the lights dim to appreciate the sunset.

Funny when I thought about it. It was sunset in Dublin; but we were traveling back in time to New York. I would be landing in New York almost at the same time I left Dublin. And from New York I planned on popping my luggage and me to Atlanta (I'd hate to disappoint Rune).

Davet removed his sunglasses and revealed large pupils rimmed with purple. Yep! Dark Elf. Well so far...I didn't see his Sabretooth teeth yet.

"I apologize. I'm not used to a lot of light unless I'm wearing special contact lens. I brought some along for our destination," he said softly, placing his sunglasses in his hoodie and removed a contact lens case.

The male flight attendant from before pushed a beverage cart into view.

Davet ordered two white wines and handed one to me.

"I hope you don't mind. You look like a woman who enjoys her wines. I am an amateur ice-wine maker." Davet said raising his plastic cup in toast.

Now that fascinated me.

"Really? What's ice-wine?"

Davet actually smiled, obviously happy to be asked.

Ok. I'm a sucker for flight conversation. Normally I don't bring anyone along to chat with. This time I felt like had with Davet as a travel companion.

I bet I could get Rune to travel with me. OK! Now my mind wandered to Rune waiting on me. And quickly my fantasy went downhill when I remembered Davet.

Rudely I took out my phone to send a text to Rune as a heads up.

I think I found the match. He's with me now. I'll see you tonight, the text said and I hit send.

"Sorry. I was letting my boyfriend know I wouldn't be arriving alone." I apologized putting my phone back in my carry-on.

"Do you live with him?" Davet asked in surprise.

"No." I blurted out abruptly. I quickly amended. "We go back and forth. He lives in Atlanta and I travel a lot."

"I see. Makes a relationship hard." Davet said agreeably.

I tried not to eye him suspiciously. I didn't expect sympathy from a Dark Elf. Maybe they had vulnerability issues when they were looking for a mate.

"I can understand the issues of relationships. Mortal relationships have their complexities." Davet responded probably reading my face.

"So you were saying that you live in Iceland making your wine. Tell me more about your life in Iceland." I said to engage Davet again.

We chatted about Iceland until we landed in New York. Then we found a crowd of people heading to the subway so I could pop us and my bags to Rune's front door.

Rune's porchlight was on. I hoped he got my text and he wasn't waiting inside naked with a bottle of wine.

I knocked on the red door and waited. Davet stood behind me on the step below me.

Rune swung open his front door all-smiles.

"Welcome home!" Rune greeted, giving me a big hug and a kiss like he hadn't seen me all week.

"Welcome to my home, sir!" Rune added cheerfully to Davet next.

"Have you been drinking?" I asked under my breathe in Greek.

"No, baby. I'm so excited to meet my first male Dark Elf." Rune said taking my hand to pull me inside so Davet could come in too.

We all got into Rune's front room and Rune had some wine and cheese set out – Greek wine and cheese by the way.

"Rune, this is Davet. Davet, this is my boyfriend Rune Kalakos." I introduced the two men to each other after I sat down to pour me some wine.

Davet sat on Rune's loveseat and Rune sat beside me on the couch.

"You are both love Jinn?" Davet uttered in surprise.

Yeah! I know...the odds.

"We are but Jinx is running point on this. I'm just hoping to reverse a former wrong I did by helping." Rune nodded, pouring a glass of wine for Davet.

"Davet here makes wine, Rune." I interjected, plucking a piece of cheese off the cheeseboard.

That started an hour-long conversation. I sat there listening and waiting for my moment.

I had no idea what time it was by the time they stopped talking for a breather.

"So when will she be here?" Davet asked on his third glass of wine.

"She won't be here until we're sure you are the right match." I finally got to say. Honestly I didn't have a clue how to locate Sigyn again. I hadn't worked on that yet.

"How do we do that? Do you have the Book of Years?" Davet asked seriously, looking from me to Rune.

"Book of Years?" Rune and I repeated in confusion. Ok. I didn't think of this part either.

I mean did I think that a male Dark Elf would find me? No. But I also didn't think a lot of things would happen to me and they have.

Davet stared back at us expectantly.

"Not a problem. I'll call Conrad. He hasn't done anything to remedy this." Rune said seemingly in control. I was quietly freakin' out because I should have planned this better.

Rune gave me another kiss and walked back to his kitchen.

Davet and I could hear Rune talking to someone in Greek I understood what Rune was saying and he wasn't asking.

A few minutes later I caught Rune walking down the hall to the front door. He opened the front door and strolled back into the living room. After him appeared who must have been Conrad.

Conrad wasn't what I expected. Obviously I wasn't what he expected because he stepped back when he saw me.

Conrad was built like Bruce Banner in The Avengers. He was tall with a mop of brown curls with blonde highlights. In his mop of hair sat a pair of wire-framed spectacles. He was wearing a red dress shirt with the sleeves rolled up to his elbows and gray slacks. Sneakers were on his feet and I was completely at a loss figuring him out.

"I suppose if a Jinn had to become a female you are the most lovely specimen to behold." Conrad said in Greek and it did sound whiney.

I could see why his voice was so surprising though. It didn't sound like it came from him.

"Do you say that to every female Jinn you meet?" I asked back in Greek.

I glanced down at his hands. He was holding a little book in his mildly calloused hands. He had the hands of a worker; but what did he do for a living?

"No. Most of your sex makes me suspicious. I think there was a line in a James Bond movie where it was said that you were a pleasurable pursuit for disposal. I tend to agree." Conrad stated finally, noticing Davet who sat there patiently.

"Now to why I was called. Of course I was in the middle of something and I hope I can return to it quickly enough." Conrad added, clearing his throat before he placed the book on the coffee

227

table. He took stole a piece of cheese, savored it and took another.

"Please. There will be other hands of poker, Conrad." Rune tutted, re-filling his glass of wine.

Conrad went into the kitchen to retrieve his own glass kind of like Grey would at my place. He got a glass, came back and filled it.

"We need to all speak in Elfish or Icelandic for Davet. We are here for his benefit." I told the two Greeks.

Rune sat back down on the couch next to me.

"Do you have the Book of Years?" Davet asked us again.

Conrad gestured to the little book on the table.

"There you are. It's just in a compact form." Conrad added sipping his wine.

I pulled the book towards us on the couch. I opened it and it grew in size where Rune had to save the bottle of wine.

Inside were yucky things. There were bits of hair; some with blood dried to it, some with skin. There was skin with blood and without. It was hella nasty. I wouldn't touch it again.

"The Book of Years! This is a pristine copy!" Davet explained bringing the book closer to him (which was fine by me).

"I'm glad you like it. It's on loan." Conrad remarked glancing over at me. I caught him out of the corner of my eyes.

"So what are we to do with the book, Davet?" Rune asked so I didn't.

"This will prove I'm worthy to approach Sigyn." Davet answered still flipping the nasty pages.

"This is the record of all bloodlines in Dark Elf history." I said catching on. I hoped I didn't wrinkle my nose or look too disgusted.

Davet and Conrad nodded.

"I shall use the most proven method of identification." Davet told us. I was suddenly afraid to know what he meant.

TWENTY-SEVEN

Davet took out a razor blade from somewhere on his person (Didn't I say terrorist?) and cut the tip of his left ring finger. Blood welled up the color of ink (interesting).

"Do you mind?" Davet asked the three of us, gesturing to the Book of Years.

"Proceed." Conrad said waving his free hand dismissively.

I'm glad he knew what to say because like I said, I didn't want to know what would happen next. I didn't like blood too much. Other class-mates became nurses and I became a wedding planner.

Davet muttered in Elfish his offering of blood proof that he was worthy of a descendant of Jupiler (whoever that was). And if he wasn't worthy for the Years to prove otherwise.

A drop of inky blood left Davet's finger and hit the page of the book Davet was reading. We watched as the page absorbed the blood like a scene from Harry Potter. Then the pages started flapping back and forth before they stopped on a blank page.

"Son of Erade, Jupiler is not your fate," a voice erupted from the book.

I almost jumped into Rune's lap but his hand was holding my right thigh down.

"Erade? I always thought I was from Jupiler's line?" Davet inquired dumbfounded.

Oh crap! I could see my plan failing before my very eyes.

"Hence the Book of Years since you crazy Elfs can't raise your *own* children." Conrad remarked smugly.

I put my face in my hands that were shaking now.

"Son of Erade should wait for a daughter of Ikonis. It is said. It is the will of the Dark Queen," the book advised next before it revealed the tree of Erade.

It was gnarly small tree and a little bud popped up showing Davet's name.

The book didn't show us Ikonis' tree.

"The Book of Years won't show Ikonis' tree until her descendant provides a sample." Conrad confirmed what I thought.

"So is Sigyn a descendant of Ikonis?" Davet and Rune asked me next.

Bail!

"Wow! It's late! We should contact Sigyn in the morning! That way we'll be rested!" I expelled with an exaggerated yawn, struggling to my feet because I did feel wobbly.

"I didn't expect to stay overnight…" Davet said looking a little uncomfortable.

"Please feel free to stay in my guest room. We'll have you home on the morrow." Rune expressed genially, standing up to escort Davet upstairs.

They went upstairs leaving me with Conrad.

"You don't have a clue what to do, do you? You should have left this one alone." Conrad said arrogantly. I suppose arrogance was a qualifying trait for a Jinn protector.

"I'm not a coward like the rest of you." I retorted just as arrogantly, cutting my eyes at him.

"Arrogance doesn't become you, little Jinn. But keep the book in case that witch turns up." Conrad scoffed, disappearing with a final laugh.

I locked up and went up to Rune's room.

Rune was waiting for me, half naked on his bed.

I glanced back across the hall and Rune's bedroom door closed with a vacuum seal.

"I don't want to talk. I don't want to hear about any problems. I just want you to come here." Rune said in Far'si and my heart went into overdrive.

My feet moved whether I wanted them to or not. Soon I stood between his legs and then I was on my knees.

"Do what you wish and I will show you what love can be between us," he added again in Far'si.

"What I wish?" I repeated, trying to think of something that I wouldn't normally do.

What would Violet do? The only reason I thought of Violet is because she told me several times about scenes from Shades of Grey.

Suddenly I had a pair of handcuffs in my hand. Both Rune and I looked down at my handcuffs. Then we glanced at Rune's solid headboard. I blinked and the headboard suddenly had spindles for handcuffs.

"You are a genius!" I laughed pushing Rune onto his back.

Then we were having a lot of fun until Davet knocked on the door.

"I thought he couldn't hear us…" I gasped pushing Rune off of me and grabbing at whatever fabric I could to cover myself.

"He can't. It must be something else." Rune hissed, clambering off his bed. He grabbed his jeans and T-shirt, throwing them on before he cracked open the door.

Sigyn came to mind. I glanced at Rune's phone on the alarm clock charger. Two-fifteen in the morning. Then again villains didn't keep normal hours, did they?

I didn't hear what Davet said but I saw Rune scrub his face. In other words it wasn't good.

Rune stepped back from the door to look at me.

"The police are here. Davet saw them from the window. I have to go downstairs. Stay here," he said to me devoid of all emotion except fright.

"No. I'm coming with you." I stated getting out of the bed to find my clothes.

Rune didn't wait on me. He went downstairs while I dressed.

I came down the stairs right into despair.

"Mr. Kalakos, please place your wrists out in front of you. You have been read your rights and you're currently out on bail," one

233

Atlanta police officer was saying to Rune. He was about the size of Thorin Oakenshield which really got on my nerves immediately.

Some dwarf was arresting my baby for what?

Rune put his wrists together in front of the officer's face – the same wrists I had handcuffed to the bed an hour ago (the ones he escaped from using his magic).

I was frozen in a bad way on the fifth step.

Rune turned his head, spying me there.

"Can my girlfriend get me some shoes or sandals? I really don't want to go out again barefoot like the last time," he asked the two officers politely.

The dwarf looked at the taller dwarf (do they have tall police officers?) before he said yeah, sure in his Atlanta drawl.

"Your shoes? That's what you want?" I blurted out, finally able to speak.

"What are you arresting him for now?" I demanded not moving down the stairs or up them.

"Ma'am, please calm down," the taller dwarf officer said softly, stifling a yawn.

"I'm always calm, Officer. I want to know why you're arresting him." I said and oddly I was calm. I just didn't have control over my voice when I was frozen to one spot.

"The death of Vong Seu Lee." Rune answered me, gazing up at me in a sad pitiful manner.

My heart sank. Sigyn was still at work. I could feel it. This had to be her doing.

"I'll get your slippers so they're easier to replace." I said flatly, forcing myself to go back up to his bedroom for his leather slides.

It took me ten minutes to bring them back because I couldn't stop crying helplessly. Not too long ago we were happily making love and now...

I handed the slides to Rune before I remembered he was handcuffed. So I placed them in front of his feet and he stepped into them. Then I just stared at his feet.

"We'll let you say goodbye, Mr. Kalakos. Understand that your bail has been revoked due to these charges," the taller dwarf said more for my benefit than Rune's.

The two officers stepped out onto the front stoop but didn't go much further.

"Rune..." I whispered beginning to cry again.

"Shh..." Rune whispered back, picking up my chin with his handcuffed hands.

He was crying too.

"I love you Jinx Hedayat. You will figure this out. You are by far the best little love Jinn. I'm so glad I met you and fell in love with you." Rune whispered in Greek.

"I will get you out of this. I will fix everything so we can live our lives and be happy." I stated feeling confident in his love.

"Good because my life in Atlanta will be done. Do you love me, Jinx? I need to hear you say it." Rune chuckled feebly, searching my eyes.

"By all of the Gods of all of the worlds I love you, Rune. There is no one else." I said sincerely, taking his hands in mine.

Rune smiled where the tears ran down and around his mouth. He leaned down and kissed me sweetly.

"I'm ready to go, officers." Rune sighed, stepping away from me.

I didn't want to see him put in the police car so I waited a sufficient amount of time before I shut the front door.

When I looked up the stairs and considered going to bed Davet was standing there.

"He appeared to be such a nice young man." Davet uttered in Elfish.

"Rune is a good man. He's innocent. We're going to fix this. Go back to bed. I have a call to make." I said seriously back in Elfish.

Davet inclined his head and disappeared into the guest room.

I sat down on the bottom step, crying some more. But not so much about Rune but in frustration. How was I going to find Sigyn? Any minute Rune spends in prison is a minute too long.

The sun was creeping into the front windows and the hallway when I picked up my head.

I just kept thinking how to find Sigyn. How did she find me? How did she contact me? How, how, how!

Then duh!

"Davet! Davet!" I shouted, rushing up the stairs.

I was about to bang on the door when he threw it open, alarmed.

"Sorry. I didn't mean to scare you. I just had a stupid question about Dark Elfs. It's a myth I

236

heard and I couldn't sleep without knowing." I said anxiously, then calming down a little.

Davet's eyes seemed to get wider.

"Are you insinuating that you can't sleep under the same roof as a Dark Elf for fear we'll creep into your dreams?"

I knew it!

"No I was actually told that Dark Elfs could if they wanted." I said flashing a smile at Davet as if my face hadn't lit up enough.

"Oh good because I have never done that to a complete stranger. Besides you and your beau are helping me." Davet pouted a little, closing the door slightly.

I thanked him and shut myself in Rune's bedroom.

I found some of my pajamas in Rune's dresser. I put them on, catching a whiff of Rune's laundry detergent. A sob caught in the back of my throat that I swallowed before I laid down in Rune's bed.

"I won't let you go like Andrea." I said to Rune's pillows.

I must have been really tired because I found myself dreaming that I was sitting at that hotel bar in San Diego. I guess I was thinking about the first time I met Sigyn.

I sat there at the bar with my glass of wine, patiently waiting and quietly thinking about Sigyn.

"Let me guess. You're here to plea for Rune's pardon."

Finally she appeared sitting next to me.

"Actually I'm here to see you." I stated simply, sipping my Moscato.

"Why would you want to see me?" Sigyn asked after the bartender brought her a drink.

"Because it has come to my attention that I owe you a debt. Rune owed you a debt too but he's in jail right now and couldn't be here. So I'm here to apologize for me and for Rune." I answered hoping I sounded sincere.

Sigyn made a huff without any words.

"Did you think an apology would appease me?" she finally said.

"No but I thought I'd get that out of the way first." I shrugged casually. I was really hoping I was peaking her interest.

"You are way too polite to be a female Jinn." Sigyn laughed.

Well at least she was amused.

"And I'm glad you came. Have you ever consulted the Book of Years?" I asked while I had her entertained.

Then Sigyn choked on her drink.

I glanced over at her, offering her a cocktail napkin.

"The Book of Years? How..." Sigyn uttered.

"Unlike my comrades and predecessors I chose to help you. Rune helped by getting a copy of the Book. I want to help you because no one should be turned away." I responded pushing my glass aside to really look at her.

Sigyn looked a little like a Betty Page drawing. I'm not sure if she looked like that at our first meeting; but then again I was creeped out and pissed off.

"You don't know what you're talking about." Sigyn recovered with a scoff.

"But I do. I have the Book of Years on Rune's coffee table. I know you will duel for superior position. I know that the bloodlines have to be similar." I said confidently, watching her take in my words.

"And you are going to find my mate for me? Are you going to charge me?" Sigyn asked suspiciously, gazing down into her drink.

"How can I charge you? I owe you. Will you please just give me a chance? I'm only asking that you give me a few minutes of your time to consult the Book." I said solemnly.

"I will give you a few minutes. I will meet you in Rune's living room." Sigyn said and left.

I woke up and ran into the door, trying to get downstairs fast. I'm an idiot I know. I was just so excited that Sigyn was willing to entertain me.

I slid down the stairs and burst into the living room.

Sigyn was sitting on the couch, staring at the Book of Years.

"You are here to witness?" she asked me without looking at me.

I nodded knowing she didn't need me to speak.

Sigyn began to mutter the same words Davet had. She added the family name of Erade where Davet had said Jupiler. I kinda stumbled back in preparation for the Book to do its thing.

She had already cut her finger and dropped the inky blood onto the paper full of other bloody stains when the Book began its erratic creepy behavior.

"Daughter of confusion, you can have any male. The blood of two strong families run through you; however the one you seek is a son of Erade. The daughter of Ikonis and Erade needs to seek the son of your cousin," the creepy voice told Sigyn. I swear the pages stopped on the same page as it did for Davet.

Sigyn sucked the rest of the blood from her fingertip taking in the Book's advice.

"Jinx? Jinx! Are you here? There's an intruder in the house!" Davet shouted sliding down the stairs too and running into me.

Sigyn shot to her feet immediately spying Davet.

The two Dark Elfs stared at each other for a couple minutes. I stood between them awkwardly, wondering if they'd duke it out right here.

"You did it," they both uttered staring at me.

I did it?

"He's my cousin." Sigyn said pointing at Davet.

"You're the daughter of Ikonis." Davet said with a slow smile.

"So...?" I urged waiting on the duel thing.

"Do you accept the duel?" Sigyn asked Davet from her position in the living room.

"I accept. What weapon do you chose?" Davet replied sounding confident and certain. I was betting he was freaking out.

"Dual edged phuniel. And where should we duel?" Sigyn told Davet way too confident.

Davet looked impressed with her choice of weapon.

"There's a fjord near Isafjorour. Meet there..."

"This afternoon at four Icelandic time. I don't want to wait another day." Sigyn added.

Thank you! I don't want to wait another day either.

"I'll meet you there. I must prepare." Davet said with a bow, disappearing from the hallway.

So I was left with just Sigyn. Man! I needed a chai tea!

A glass appeared in my empty hands. Damn! It was good to be a Jinn!

TWENTY-EIGHT

I would like for you to witness our duel. It is a privilege and will authenticate our union." Sigyn said approaching me.

"I would love that. After all you are now one of my clients. I would want to see it through to conclusion and then some." I smiled so happy for my tea and a possible end in sight.

Sigyn might have smiled…possibly.

"There's not any way that this can fall through, right?" I asked what just popped into my head. OK. I was a little skeptical because this was too easy.

"He accepted the duel. I picked a simple weapon. He just has to know when to submit." Sigyn stated as if it's a no-brainer.

Then she disappeared, leaving me alone.

I finished my tea, sent a text to Violet that she could move on with *her* to do list, and then I took a little nap.

When I woke up I found some more jeans that might have been clean in my suitcase. I grabbed another sweater, put on my boots and pea coat, and I was ready to go. I just had to hope I didn't oversleep for four Icelandic time. I glanced down at my phone as I slipped it into my pocket. I would be right on time.

I wished to be exactly where Sigyn and Davet were (like I would be able to locate the exact fjord near some crazy named town) and disappeared from Rune's townhouse.

I re-appeared in a gust of freezing wind. Holy crap! Was this spring in the Arctic?

I surveyed my surroundings to find Davet and Sigyn preparing for their duel.

"You made it, Jinn!" Sigyn called to me before she came over to me carrying a long staff from the looks of it.

The sun was behind them, preparing to set. Then I remembered that the sun didn't exactly set up here. It just hovered on either horizon unable to make up its mind.

Sigyn stopped in front of me handing me a small chalkboard with a piece of chalk. The staff was actually only four feet long with two feet of blade on each end.

"I want you to count Davet's strikes on me. Can you do that for me, little Jinn?" she asked me, doing a side stretch.

"Sure." I said a little confused by the request. Tally Davet's strikes? Huh?

Sigyn bowed and went back to her position.

Davet didn't even look over at me. I suppose he was just so intent on focusing on this duel he didn't want to be distracted.

"Ready?" Sigyn hollered over at Davet in Elfish.

Davet hollered back 'proceed' and they began.

I took out my phone to snap some quick pics for Arabella (least I could do for her help) while it was still safe.

Then the duel really began. Davet attacked with his phuniel spinning like a baton. When he was close enough Sigyn jabbed at him with one end of her phuniel. Davet backflipped like a gymnast away from her attack without a scratch. Sigyn started the next attack doing an aerial cartwheel with her phuniel jabbing and slashing when she landed. Davet bobbed and weaved like a boxer before he spun and flipped over Sigyn. He pinned her to his chest using the phuniel as a chest bar. She swung her head back to headbutt him; but his head moved to bite her on the neck.

When he bit her I finally noticed his lower fangs. They were like needles and like vampires in Van Helsing. Eek!

His bite infuriated Sigyn (I think) because she let out this loud roar unlike anything I had ever heard a human do.

She brought down her phuniel between her legs to cut his shin.

Davet roared back at her, pushing her away to counter. As she spun around for the attack he used one edge to cut her from her left collarbone diagonally to just below her right breast.

"Oh no!" I gasped dropping the chalkboard and chalk.

"That's all you got?" Sigyn roared back at her opponent.

I scrambled to pick up the chalkboard and find the chalk. Obviously she was alright...bloody but alright.

Davet used his phuniel to catapult him into Sigyn where he kicked her in her injury.

I found the chalk marking the strike. He was definitely on the defense; which I think made him the aggressor and the more dominant. I wasn't sure if Sigyn had planned for that.

Sigyn grunted and fell back, clutching her chest.

"Are you saying I don't need this breast?" she growled at him in Elfish.

"All I did was add to its beauty! You're the one who chose the weapon!" Davet retorted spinning his phuniel in front of him.

Might I add that they weren't dueling in armor plating or heavy padding or even jeans and sweaters?

Apparently Dark Elfs dueled in lightweight transparent black material. It almost looked like they were dueling in pajamas. And here they were in a freezing fjord in Iceland's version of spring. Arabella definitely didn't mention this.

Sigyn gave him a nasty glare as the inky blood seeped into her black top.

"Attack why don't you?" she snapped at him, getting to her feet.

She stood up and wobbled before she fell to one knee. I winced.

"Do you submit?" Davet asked not approaching.

Yeah he's right. It could have been a trick.

"It's too soon to submit." Sigyn remarked willing herself to stand again. This time she planted one end of the phuniel in the frozen ground to hoist herself up. She leaned against it once she was up.

"The sooner you submit, the sooner we can move on with our lives." Davet said exactly what I was thinking.

Sigyn held up her right hand to catch her breathe.

Her hair had come undone from her high bun. Some of it was on her shoulders, some of it was still up.

Honestly she looked a mess.

Davet looked sweaty and that's all. His hair was still tightly braided. His clothes were still in one piece. Oops! I take that back. A few strands of hair had fallen into his face.

"I don't know what happens next." Sigyn uttered in Russian talking to herself.

"Love." I told her since I understood Russian and I was close by.

"How many strikes?" she asked me in a pant, touching the location of the bite.

"Including counters...four at least." I answered consulting the chalkboard.

Then Sigyn fell flat on her back unconscious.

This time I abandoned the chalkboard to go to Sigyn's side. I didn't know what just happened and that scared me. Had she just died?

Davet waited a few minutes before he approached.

"What happened?" I asked him in Elfish.

"She's fine. It will be easier to transport her if she's a little groggy." Davet shrugged, jamming one end of his weapon into the ground. He squatted down on the other side of Sigyn's prone body.

"From blood loss?" I asked wishing that her wounds would heal for my benefit and possibly hers.

"From the bite." Sigyn whispered.

I had this look of 'huh' on my face.

"She's right. She's groggy from the bite. My saliva has a numbing agent that empties through my lower canines." Davet nodded, reaching down to touch Sigyn's face.

It appeared to be a gentle touch.

"Did you know that?" I leaved closer to ask Sigyn.

"There is much I didn't count on when a little Jinn I harbored a grudge against decided to help me," she whispered again.

"Can I leave her with you safely? You won't kill her, will you?" I asked Davet next who had picked up my chalkboard somehow.

"She had you mark my strikes?" he asked me, pointing to my tallies.

"I just did what a spectator should." I smiled awkwardly.

"You wouldn't submit until there was more than two strikes, would you?" Davet grinned down at Sigyn.

She tried to shake her head; but it just flopped to the side.

"We shall go to my home close to here and start on these four. Maybe the Dark Queen will let us keep two." Davet replied to Sigyn and me.

Then he picked up Sigyn from the ground, slinging her over his shoulder.

"I thank you so much, Jinx Hedayat for finding my mate. I've waited three centuries to find the right one and all it took was a web site from you. You will hold a special place of honor in our home always." Davet said sincerely with a bow.

I bowed and when I looked up they were gone, leaving only their phuniels.

I stood there for a couple minutes trying to figure out what just happened.

Were the four tallies to become four children? He said he'd go home and start on these four?

TWENTY-NINE

Well I pondered that until I realized that...duh...it's freezing in Iceland. So I went home but I mean my home. I figured for the last part of my plan I didn't need to be in Atlanta. But then I remembered that my car was at JIA so I decided to pop up at JIA with my bags and all.

No one was going to notice that a Middle Eastern girl just magically appeared in an airport garage. If they did...oh well!

I trudged up to my car (I didn't have to locate it this time because I made sure I appeared a short distance from it) with my Jansport luggage behind me. I popped the trunk with my keyless remote, tossed in my luggage, slammed the trunk closed and walked around to the drivers' side. Before I could push the little button on the door handle the door opened and pushed out.

"What the..." I uttered stepping back against another Nissan...a Quest parked beside me.

"You didn't wish for that to happen. No one's died in your car to possess it. So it can only mean one thing..." Grey remarked in that cocky sort of way of his. He pushed the door open further.

"That I'm stupid or you've broke into my car. But that's two things, isn't it?" I quipped regaining control of my heart. He scared the crap out of me.

"Just get in." Grey grumbled, obviously not wanting to play the game of wit and sarcasm (probably too advanced for him).

"It's amazing where all of that sass comes from and then you switch to charm," he added while I climbed behind the wheel. The last time Grey approached me at the airport he stole my keys in order to convince me that I was a Jinn. I then tested his theory by depositing his ass behind my car, retrieving my keys and leaving him in my dust. At least that's how I remember it.

"It's a gift." I remarked sitting there looking at him.

"Go on home. We can talk while you drive." Grey said buckling his seat belt.

"What's there to talk about?" I asked starting the car.

I backed out of the spot and headed to the ticket booth to pay for my car's stay in the lot.

"You did what no one else would." Grey said. By his tone I wasn't sure if this was a good thing or a bad.

"If you are referring to Sigyn then yes I did." I said in response.

"Why?"

"Because what you all did was wrong. It didn't make sense to me to follow in your footsteps."

"Did you do it to get paid?" Grey asked pretty much insulting me.

We were almost to the parking attendant when I slammed on my brakes, jerking him ion his seatbelt.

"I might not give refunds if you ignore my advise; but who would I be if I charged someone I had ignored before?" I snapped glaring at him before I continued on to the booth.

Grey shrugged. "It was a sensible question."

"You know I'm really thinking that you had a bunch of self-centered assholes like yourself before me. But I'll tell you this...I'm not them. I'm Jinx Marni Hedayat and I have a conscience." I continued my rant while I opened the window and snatched my purse from the backseat (where Grey had tossed it when I got in).

"Marni?" Grey scoffed wrinkling his nose bridge.

I paid the attendant, took my receipt for my billing and flashed a smile at the attendant. Then I rolled up the window and glared at Grey.

"I felt like having a middle name when I applied for my business license. Thank you very much." I retorted caught up in my attitude. But I seriously did give myself a middle name. Marni sounded American but not and it started with an M like most people.

Grey laughed for a few minutes, amused again by my antics.

"Seriously now...you helped Sigyn and for what?" Grey said after he had his laugh.

"Well I was considering wishing back to life and health all of those affected by the lens she sold to Rune." I replied arrogantly. I hadn't told

251

anyone my end game until just now. I liked how it sounded out loud. Amazingly it didn't sound stupid.

"And what about Rune?" Grey waited to ask when I had gotten on I 95 South.

There was intermittent traffic and what's worse is that I had no clue what day it was. The console digital clock said it was a little after ten-thirty Eastern time. Not knowing the day was disorienting just so you know.

I shrugged. I kinda hoped that fixing his clients would help Rune. But was I going to tell that to Grey?

No.

"Does my idea sound like it will work? It's not frowned upon if I help Rune, is it?" I inquired to keep him from asking anything else about Rune.

"I will say that your idea sounds a whole lot better than your one to save Andrea. And as long as it's done in the name of love I don't think they'll call us into the headmaster's office." Grey replied. But why did he sound like he wanted to add a 'but'?

So I waited to see if he would add what he wanted to add.

Grey stayed quiet until we were passing the Zoo Parkway.

"He deserves something good to happen for him."

"Something good…" I repeated fishing for Grey's definition. I mean he was talking like Rune was his buddy and his buddy had fallen on hard times.

Rune had but I'm here for him.

"I know you're trying to hide your feelings for him but it's not necessary." Grey added simply as we went up the steep incline that was the Dames Point Bridge (it was the only bridge Jacksonville had that was *just* tall enough for a small cruise ship to pass under).

I didn't know how to respond to that so I drove.

"I think he might deserve someone as special as my charge but I'm not really sure," he continued. This time he sounded phony.

"What is your problem, Grey? I have a father to give me advise and you're not buddy-buddy with Rune so come off it." I scoffed.

"Actually if I ever had a friend it was Rune. Then we lost touch like we tend to do. Besides I want good things for my comrades even if he's a love Jinn now." Grey shrugged casually.

"You are so full of crap, Grey. Just stick to the Jinn advice and keeping me safe. All right?" I actually laughed.

When he didn't respond I peeked over to see that he'd done the Grey thing and disappeared.

Anyway I got home, dragged myself into the house and fell into bed with Damascus (who didn't move over).

The next morning which was a Saturday (according to my iPhone) I woke up and made my wish like I told Grey I would. Then I started my day like every other day, thinking about Rune.

I know I sounded heartless yesterday; but I really did care about Rune. Truthfully I was crazy about Rune Kalakos.

"I know...I'm frustrated too. Do I do an indoor wedding or outdoor wedding?" Violet expelled from her desk after I had sighed for the hundredth time at my desk.

"I'm not listening to you because if I do I'll end up planning it." I said putting my fingers in my ears.

To ease my stress I decided to call Jill at Rune's studio (I still had Rune's business card). Of course as soon as I dialed a call from Tamara in Rock Hill came through.

"Hey Tamara! Is something wrong?" I responded cheerfully, checking my Outlook calendar, my planner app and my planner.

"I think I found a caterer. Can you meet us Monday?" Tamara said anxiously. Almost every time I talked to Tamara she sounded like it was an emergency.

This time however she had every right to be. Billy wanted a say in the caterer so the decision hadn't been made.

I said one moment while I checked Tuesday's and Wednesday's to-do lists. I figured I needed two days to tidy up Billy and Tamara's wedding.

"I can be there tomorrow. Should I call you when I land?" I said optimistically, opening my checklist template so I could update and print for my trip.

Violet scooted over in her chair when she heard 'land'. I was thinking about popping up to

South Carolina and popping back without spending money on a flight; but my accountant would wonder why my travel expenses had gone down.

Tamara said yes so I promised I would, then we hung up.

"I need a round trip ticket, hotel and rental car for Charlotte for tomorrow and Monday." I told Vi, hitting print on my template.

"On it!" Violet announced startling Damascus on the loveseat.

While she did that I got out Damascus' leash and Damascus jumped up for his walk. I grabbed up my phone and we headed out.

I tried dialing Jill again. I hoped being away from my desk would allow me to avoid interruption.

After two rings Jill answered professionally.

"Kalakos Studios. This is Jill Barberie. What can we capture for you?"

"Hey Jill. It's Jinx Heydan." I said feeling a knot in my stomach (it just showed up when Jill answered).

Silence for a minute.

"Hey Miss Jinx. How are you?" Jill finally replied. I heard some shuffling and drawers closing.

"I'm OK. I was wondering if you'd heard from Rune." OK. Now that I asked that out loud it sounded as stupid.

"Well as his girlfriend I thought you would know that he was arrested the other night for another client's death," she said confirming my call was stupid.

"Yeah. I was there when they arrested him. Since then have you heard from him? Like today? I didn't want to call his phone if his phone is still at the house…" I said with a touch of attitude that even Damascus glanced back at me.

"I'm sorry, Miss Jinx. It's been a rough two days or even weeks for me. I've never worked for someone that's been accused of a crime. Mr. Kalakos…Rune…has always been so nice to me." Jill apologized.

"But I haven't heard from him today. I did talk to Mr. Carruthers who agreed to represent Rune and he said Rune refused to see him." Jill added.

"I see. Well give me a call if you hear from him. I'll try to give him a call even though they said no bail will be granted." I said stiffly, wondering if I should have made that wish to free him. How long does the justice system take to release somebody?

"Will do. Mr. Carruthers said he was going to speak with the deceased's families this week anyway. We just think Rune's given up. But I'll let you know Miss Jinx." Jill concluded as Damascus and I walked up our walkway.

I thanked her for that and went inside hanging up.

I wanted to try Rune's cell phone but no sooner did I walk back into the house then my alerts started popping up. Eleven or twelve weddings are no joke.

THIRTY

Sunday I landed in Charlotte at ten in the morning, checked into my hotel after getting my rental car (some tiny ass Escort or something) and got something to eat. I called Tamara (who was in the middle of one of her yoga classes) to tell her I was in town.

"Oh! That's awesome! Let me call Billy to see when he can meet us! I'll text you back!" she chirped before she hung up on me.

Really I was still in Charlotte but Charlotte? Rock Hill? What's the difference?

Ten minutes later she texted that Billy couldn't leave work until four-thirty with a frowny face. I sent back that it was OK. Where should we meet? Shoot! That gave me time to go shopping or do some work for the remainder of the day.

Well I had time to do both. So I worked for two hours (checking emails, doing my blog, researching). Then I went shopping for nothing in particular. I tried to think of any birthdays or anniversaries (family-wise) that I could shop for and found out on Facebook that it was my new sister in law Minau's birthday. She was kind enough to note favorite stores on her page so I did some online shopping while standing in the Northlake Mall.

But then I needed my brother Khalid's mailing address so I sent a message to Violet to have her get that for me. She responded just as quickly as I expected and I was able to ship a very nice Louis Vuitton purse to her in Karaj.

I wandered around Northlake until it was time to drive to Monroe Road and the caterer Billy picked out. I had researched a few more in Concord and one in Charlotte on Church Street. I had previous referrals for the one in Charlotte from fellow wedding planners.

"Billy's co-worker used this company for their wedding reception. She said the food was awesome." Tamara told me as we stood outside of the caterer's to wait on Billy.

"Did you decide on a cuisine?" I asked glancing behind me at the storefront. Southern cuisine had never occurred to me to be reception food. At least not for a fancy wedding (backyard wedding yes).

Tamara shrugged. Then Billy showed up and I asked him the same question.

"I figured something casual would be good. We're not extremely fancy people. Authentic down-home cooking is perfect." Billy told me, holding the store's door open for his fiancée and me.

"What the hell! Let's see what they can do." I expelled willing to go on this adventure.

Billy introduced us to the catering manager, who was more than happy to bring out a few samples for us to try.

He (the catering manager) brought out a tray of different meats with the catering menu.

"So who are you to them?" he asked me between courses (was I being too literal with that term 'courses'?).

"I'm sorry. I'm Jinx Heydan, their wedding planner. What was your name again?" I introduced myself again, although I was certain I was introduced before. But then again my mind was elsewhere. Still no call from Rune.

"Mack. Jinx? Awesome name!" the catering manager beamed.

I thanked him. Then I dug into the course of sides.

An hour later I walked out of there wanting ribs. It was weird. I had to go to the first ribs place I saw. Billy and Tamara went home with Mack's catering menu prices. They were going to call me with their opinion. We were going to meet up tomorrow for more tastings.

I was halfway through a plate of ribs when Billy called to tell me that they decided to go with Mack.

"Are you sure? We have three places to look at tomorrow." I asked, cleaning my fingers with my napkin before I pulled out the catering menu from my bag.

"The price is great. Do you think they can really come through for us?" Billy replied uncertain as always (or as long as I've been working with him).

"Let me handle that." I said cheerfully.

So Billy let me do what I did best...once I was done with my dinner.

THIRTY-ONE

I came home the next afternoon to glasses of wine already ready. Matter of fact I stepped into the house from the garage with my overnight bag over my left shoulder to find Violet waiting on me.

She handed me a glass full of sparkling Moscato eagerly.

My gaze went to Damascus sitting on his hunches next to Violet. I tried using the telepathy I didn't have to ask him what was up with Eager Emily but he didn't have an answer of course. He *did* tilt his head...possibly.

"Did you notice something on your drive in?" Violet asked brightly, toasting me with her glass.

"Yeah. Your rental car is gone." I noted hesitantly, going to my bedroom. They followed me.

I took a sip of wine while I tried to unpack and ignore them.

"Yeah. Tomorrow Kyle and I are going to pick up or sign off on my stuff. They finally arrived. But that's not it. Notice anything else?" Violet said, plopping down on my bed.

I started sorting my laundry, still ignoring them.

"The remodeled house next to the Mexicans is up for rent." I said the next thing I could think of.

I tossed aside clothes for the cleaners and when I looked up I could see an expectant look on Violet's face.

"You want to live next to the Mexicans now? I bet they have great football parties." I remarked considering the remodeled place. Really I shouldn't complain since the house I was living in now belonged to Uncle Ash's friend.

"You're close..." Violet eked out, clutching her wineglass.

Just then Kyle came in through the front door since I had closed the garage door behind me.

"I see the moving van is gone. That guy was the picture of efficiency." Kyle noted standing outside of my room because he could see Violet sitting at the end of my bed.

"Someone already moved into the house?" I asked still thinking of the house next to the Mexicans.

"Yeah. Yesterday." Kyle said like duh.

"Then they should take down the FOR RENT sign. It's misleading." I huffed standing in my doorway now to stick my tongue out at Kyle. Ew! I just got a thought! Soon he'll be my cousin in law!

Kyle looked confused. "There isn't a FOR RENT sign up anymore. Which house are you referring?"

"Which house are *you* talking about? I'm talking about the green one next to the Mexicans." I said.

"The one that was a foreclosure forever. Across the street from Mr. Michael." Kyle replied still looking at me like I'm crazy.

"I'm definitely not living behind the people that can't keep their dogs in their own yard. Damascus would get jealous and that house is smaller than this one." I responded shaking my head.

I continued to sort laundry and sip wine.

Violet continued to watch me intently.

"Don't you want to check out our new neighbor?" she finally came out and asked.

"Have I ever met any of our neighbors?" I quipped grabbing an arms full of laundry to head out to the garage and the washing machine.

"You should start." Violet piped following me but leaving Damascus behind.

I actually glared at him. If I was a dog I probably would have snarled.

Don't get me wrong. I love people. I love meeting people. I just don't do my neighbors. It could be because I was hiding out pretending my business was in someplace more classy than a rental home. I don't know. I just don't chat with my neighbors.

Anyway so Violet left it alone until the next day.

As a small businesswoman of an international company who didn't exactly observe all of my Jewish or Islamic beliefs I took days off whenever. Sometimes I took off on Wednesdays like today.

So I was off and Violet thought after having breakfast at our favorite place, the Waffle House, that we should go on a small adventure.

"Come on! It's just the wine store." Violet pleaded.

I glanced down at my phone to see no new messages from Rune and that my clock said it was five o'clock somewhere.

"Fine. Let's go." I muttered. I was getting more sad by the day. Rune hadn't sent me any texts or called so that meant he was still in prison. In prison for what? I haven't a clue since everybody should be alive and well, according to my wish.

"Why can't he just wish himself free? He can wish me a new outfit but not his ass out of jail? What's wrong with him?" I continued to rant out loud, forgetting that Violet was in the car with me.

Luckily she was singing New Edition at the top of her lungs along with the adult R&B radio station so she didn't hear me.

We got to the Town Center and the wine warehouse store (which is like a wine grocery store). I parked and we went inside. All of wines were separated by country or region. They usually had someone giving out samples too.

"I want to find some wine to bring over to the new neighbor to welcome him." Violet expressed happily, grabbing up a hand basket as we walked in.

"What's your deal with the neighbor? Don't you have a man?" I retorted suddenly thinking about Davet and his ice-wine. I wonder if they would have ice-wine here.

"Well I would prefer if you went over to meet him but you're being a butthead." Violet remarked snidely.

"What? So I can put in a good word for you?" I quipped back, looking for an Iceland sign. I was whole-heartedly searching for ice-wine to sample.

"I told you! You should meet him. You're single." Violet snapped obviously getting a little aggravated with me.

"I'm not single. I have a man too." I added sharply, watching Violet stalk into the Mediterranean section; in particular Greece. I loved the Greek wine I tried with Rune.

"I have a man too." I repeated with a little less attitude.

I followed her to select some wines, pointing out one that Rune had. I had less fire to fight. I wanted to hear from Rune.

So I took out my phone to call the studio again.

The phone rang and then the operator said that the number had been disconnected.

"What's wrong? Your man isn't answering?" Violet asked almost like she knew. I hadn't told her that Rune had been arrested...ever.

"He lost his phone a while ago. I wouldn't put it past him that he lost it again." I said with one of those fake smiles.

We took the hand basket full of wines, two very nice wineglasses and a meat tray to the register.

"It's a gift. Do you have any nice baskets with that plastic stuff to go over it?" Violet asked the cashier.

"Absolutely!" the girl piped holding up her arm to get someone else's attention.

She finished ringing us up and another chick came up. This chick took our purchases to another area to wrap up like Violet wanted. Then I was in charge of carrying the big basket out to my Altima.

"So do you think I could get you to take this over to the new neighbor? I mean chances are he won't even be home." Violet asked again, glancing into the backseat at the basket.

"If he's not there, can I leave it at the door with a note?" I asked in return. If she said no then I wasn't going to do it.

"Sure." Violet beamed, searching her purse for a piece of paper and a pen like I didn't have that...possibly.

I agreed to be the Good Samaritan when we got home. Which we got home soon because Violet wanted to watch a specific TV show. She hopped out of the car when I pulled into the garage.

Yep! She bailed quickly on me.

I hauled the basket out of the backseat, bumped the door closed with my hip and exhaled a heavy sigh.

I stepped to the edge of the garage, peering out across the street. I couldn't tell if the

265

new neighbor was home because he happened to be in the minority by parking in the garage. Gosh darn it!

Come on Jinx! You can do it! Think of him as a client...a new client, my conscience encouraged me.

Another huff and I stalked across the street to the sidewalk. I adjusted the basket in my arms, smoothed my hair and adjusted my red elastic headband (just in case. I didn't want to look a mess). Then I encouraged myself some more up the neighbor's walkway that had been nicely landscaped by the new owner (I had never noticed of course. Sure I took walks but I wasn't paying attention).

Adjusting the basket one more time I plastered a smile on my face and knocked. Holy crap! I knocked on this complete stranger's door like I was selling Girl Scout cookies! Eek!

Someone inside called 'Just a minute' and I wanted to drop the basket and run.

I hesitated too long to run because the door was opening too soon.

"I...uhm..." I stammered stupidly.

"Well look at this. A welcoming committee. Maybe you can tell me what day is garbage day," the guy said full of cheer.

Wait! I knew that voice!

I tore my eyes away from the basket to finally look at my new neighbor.

"R-rune?" I uttered in disbelief.

The basket felt so light in my arms suddenly when I realized that I was looking at Rune.

His mass of black hair was hidden partially behind a bandana. He had some dust on his face smeared with sweat. All sorts of crazy images popped into my head that someone else was enjoying Rune's time. Someone else was swimming in those perfect blue eyes of his.

He deftly grabbed the basket from my arms before I dropped it.

"Come in. I've been working nonstop. I thought Violet would have gotten you over here sooner." Rune smiled, gesturing that I enter. So I did.

The interior looked nothing like my place – more narrow and cozier (code word for small). The furniture wasn't the same either. His townhouse had a Victorian feel to it. This place was modern.

"I adjust with the places I fill. All except in one room." Rune smiled closing the front door as I surveyed the public spaces.

"What room is that?" I asked curiously, pretending to be an innocent neighbor.

Rune put the basket on the foyer side table. He then extended his right hand to me; which I took. My hands were shaking for some crazy reason.

I was able to hold on to his hand though as he escorted me to the master bedroom. He pushed the door open to reveal the bedroom I remembered.

"Are you trying to seduce me?" I gasped playfully, releasing Rune's hand.

"You're my girl still...aren't you?" Rune asked with a frown turning me to face him.

"I'd like to think I am; however I've been ignored for a few days by my man." I replied more like snapped. Suddenly I was a little bit angry.

Now Rune pouted.

"I told you that I would be making a change no matter the outcome. The only thing I didn't change was how I felt about you. I got out of jail when Mr. Carruthers brought the deceased to the jail to revoke their statements. Scared the shit out of everyone. I had to use magic to fix their memories. Then I figured I might as well fix everything including me. So I did and came here to conveniently rent across the street."

I winced because he was basically saying my wish was kinda, sorta half assed.

"I didn't think about the dead coming back to life part. I thought it would be more like it never happened." I said awkwardly.

"Are you still my girl?" Rune asked me in Far'si, searching my eyes again.

"I don't think I stopped." I said in kind even though I felt like such an idiot. Thanks Grey for the half-ass advice.

"My little Jinn." Rune grinned before he kissed me.

Something about how he said that sounded like he was proud that I was his little Jinn.

So yes I fell into bed with him. But after making love I laid there unable to sleep.

"What's on your mind?" Rune asked stroking my forearm that was across his chest.

"If you never existed in Atlanta what does that mean? You know for Jill and Connie and Jos?" I whispered with my thoughts racing.

"Jill woke up yesterday as the receptionist for Mr. Carruthers and as far as she's concerned she's always been there. To your clients I'm a photographer you suggested and contracted. I'm still their photographer. Go to sleep, angel," he explained softly, kissing the top of my head.

"But now what are you going to do?" I asked.

"I'll be a photographer. Maybe we can have a partnership. You know throw me a bone every now and again. Otherwise I can get a job if needed." Rune chuckled. He didn't sound in the least bit worried about his future.

"Will that make you happy though?" I continued.

"Jinx, as long as I have you my life is set," he stated.

And before I could ask another question I was out.

"Two can play at that game." Rune whispered into my dreams.

Yeah. He's right. Two could and I was happy to play the game with him.

THE END FOR NOW
04 JUL 14 5:23 EDT

23063958R00154

Printed in Great Britain
by Amazon